nickelodeon™

PANDEMONIUM!

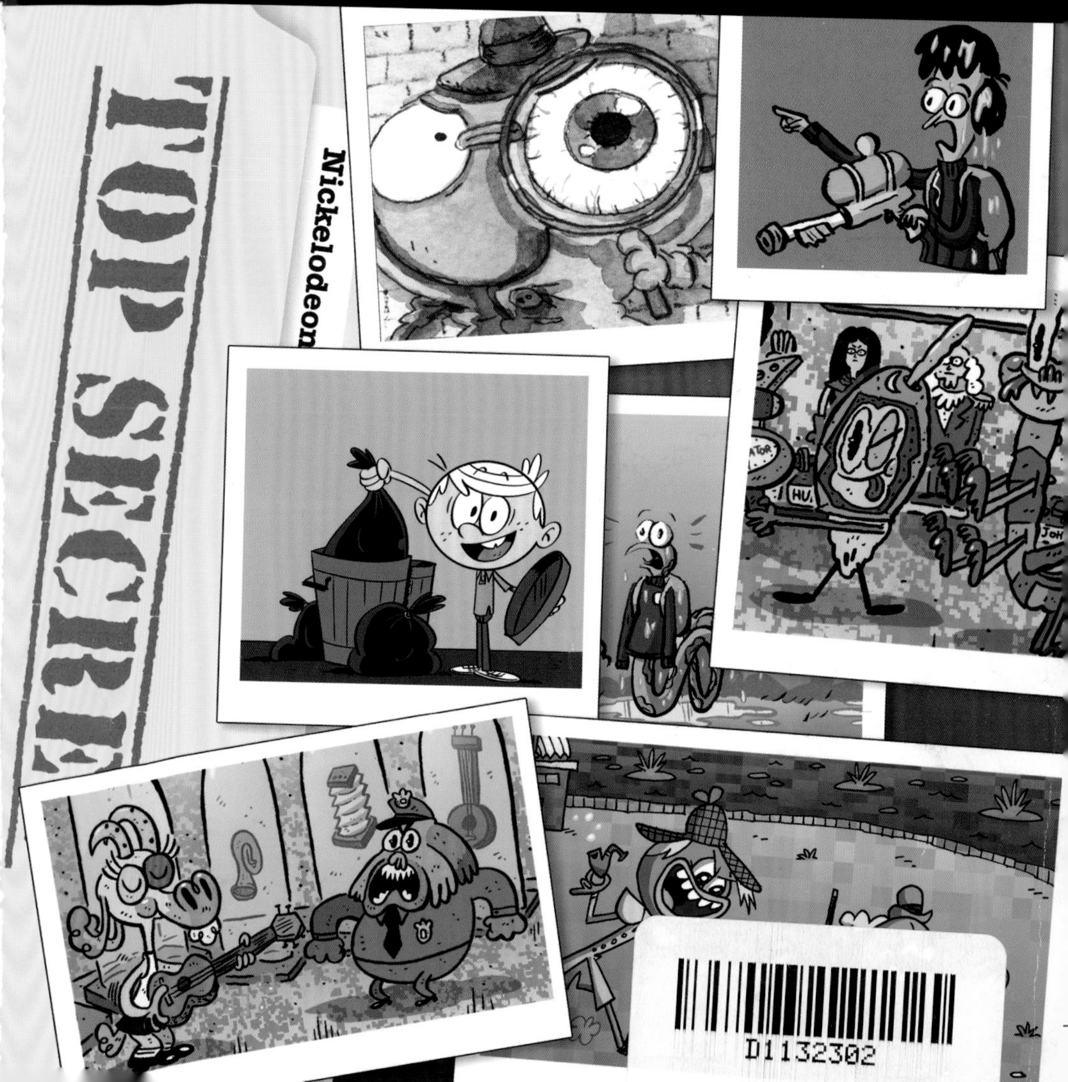
Nickelodeon

nickelodeon GRAPHIC NOVELS AVAILABLE FROM PAPERCUTZ

nickelodeon
SANJAY AND CRAIG
FIGHT THE FUTURE WITH FLAVOR!
PAPERCUTZ

SANJAY AND CRAIG
#1 "Fight the Future with Flavor"

nickelodeon
SANJAY AND CRAIG
NEW KID ON THE BLOCK
PAPERCUTZ

SANJAY AND CRAIG
#2 "New Kid on the Block"

nickelodeon
ALL NEW GRAPHIC NOVEL!
STORY TIME WITH
SANJAY AND CRAIG
PAPERCUTZ

SANJAY AND CRAIG
#3 "Story Time with Sanjay and Craig"

nickelodeon
BREADWINNERS
JOURNEY TO THE BOTTOM OF THE SEATS
PAPERCUTZ

BREADWINNERS
#1 "Journey to the Bottom of the Seats"

nickelodeon
BREADWINNERS
Buhdeuce Rocks the Rocket
PAPERCUTZ

BREADWINNERS
#2 "Buhdeuce Rocks the Rocket"

nickelodeon
PANDEMONIUM!
CHANNELING FUN
PAPERCUTZ

NICKELODEON
PANDEMONIUM #1
"Channeling Fun"

nickelodeon
PANDEMONIUM!
SPIES AND DUCKTECTIVES
TOP SECRET
PAPERCUTZ

NICKELODEON
PANDEMONIUM #2
"Spies and Ducktectives"

nickelodeon
HARVEY BEAKS
INSIDE JOKE
PAPERCUTZ

HARVEY BEAKS
#1 "Inside Joke"

nickelodeon
THE FEEL-GOOD GRAPHIC NOVEL!
HARVEY BEAKS
IT'S CRAZY TIME!
PAPERCUTZ

HARVEY BEAKS
#2 "It's Crazy Time"

nickelodeon
PIG GOAT BANANA CRICKET
Orgle Borgle Selfie Simple-Dee-Doo!
PAPERCUTZ

PIG GOAT BANANA CRICKET
#1 "Orgle Borgle Selfie Simple-Dee Doo!"

COMING SOON

nickelodeon
THE LOUD HOUSE
THERE WILL BE CHAOS
PAPERCUTZ

LOUD HOUSE #1
"There will be Chaos"

Nickelodeon graphic novels are available for $7.99 each in paperback, $12.99 each in hardcover. Available from booksellers everywhere. You can also order online from Papercutz.com, or call 1-800-886-1223, Monday through Friday, 9-5 EST. MC, Visa, and AmEx accepted. To order by mail, please add $4.00 for postage and handling for the first book ordered, $1.00 for each additional book and make check payable to NBM Publishing. Send to: Papercutz, 160 Broadway, Suite 700, East Wing, New York, NY 10038.

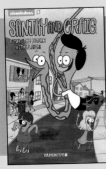

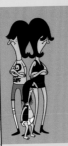

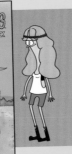

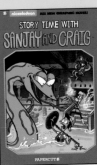

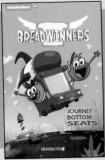

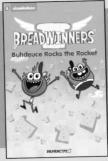

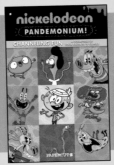

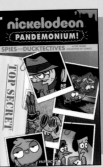

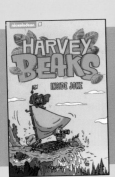

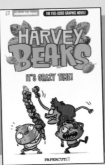

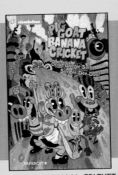

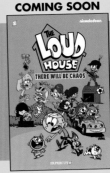

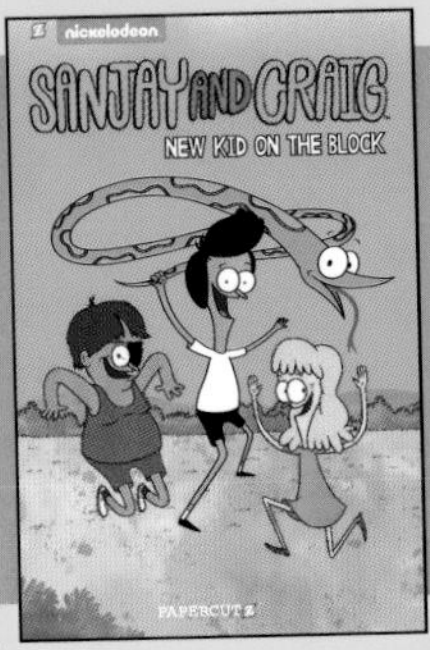

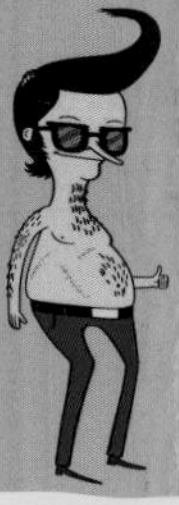

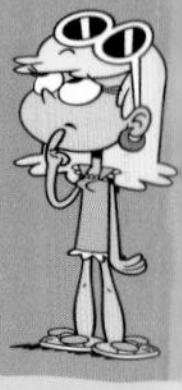

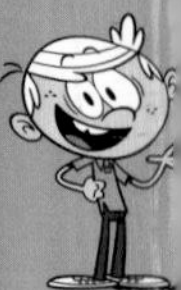

TOP SECRET

L. LOUD

H. BEAKS

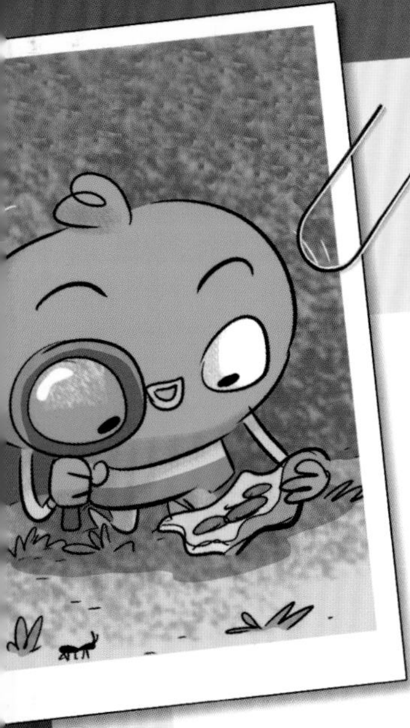

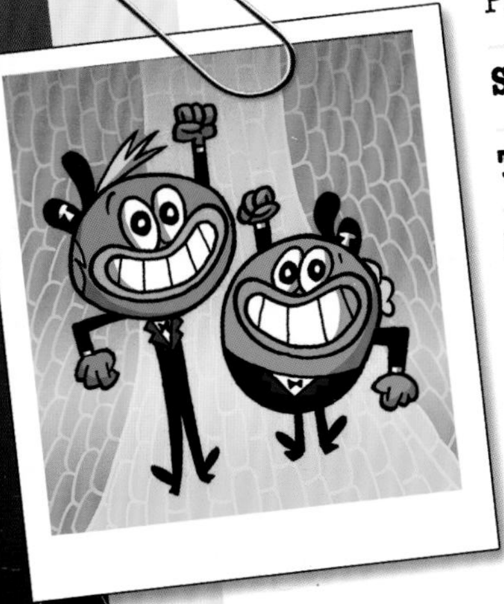

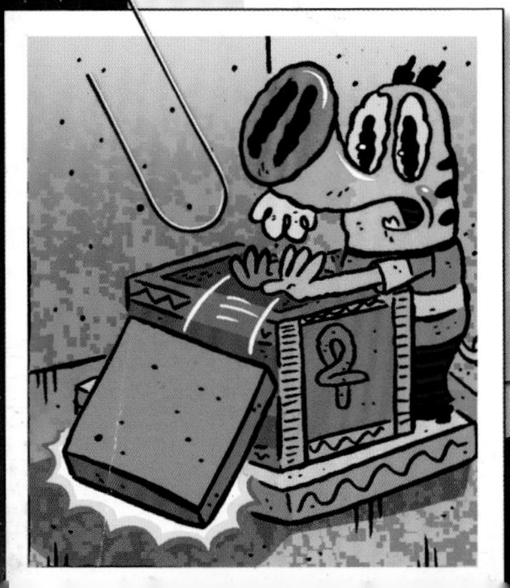

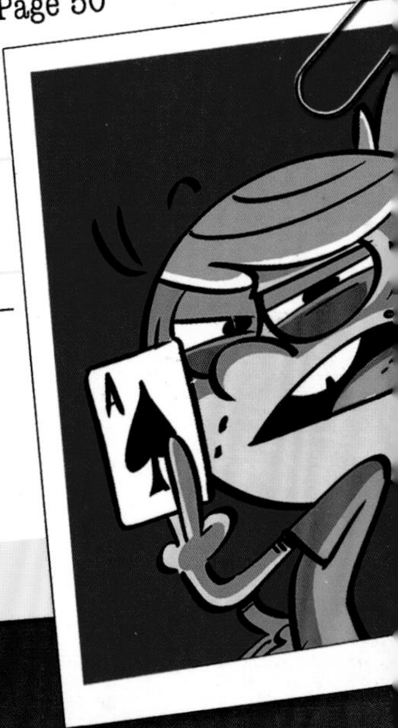
A

FOR YOUR EYES ONLY...

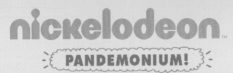

nickelodeon

PANDEMONIUM!

#2 "SPIES AND DUCKTECTIVES"

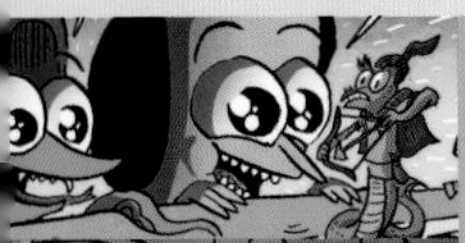

"GOBLINS AND GAZEBOS"
Eric Esquivel – Writer
Sam Spina – Artist, Letterer
Laurie E. Smith – Colorist

"THE PENSIONERS"
Eric Esquivel – Writer
Sam Spina – Artist, Letterer
Laurie E. Smith – Colorist

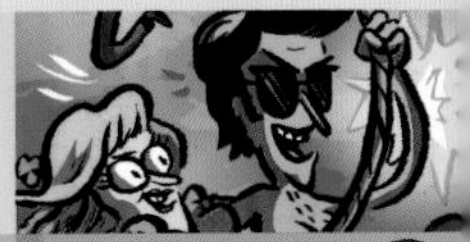

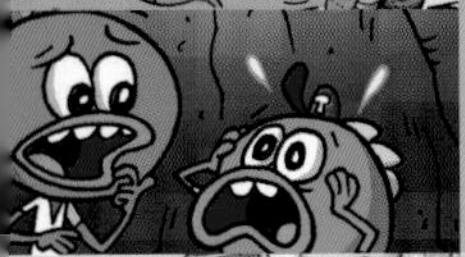

"LIVE AND LET RYE"
Eric Esquivel – Writer
Gary Fields – Artist
Laurie E. Smith – Colorist
Tom Orzechowski – Letterer

"HARVEY BEAKS: PIZZA DETECTIVE"
David Sheidt – Writer
Andreas Schuster – Artist, Letterer
Laurie E. Smith – Colorist

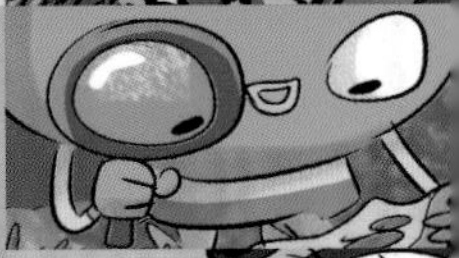

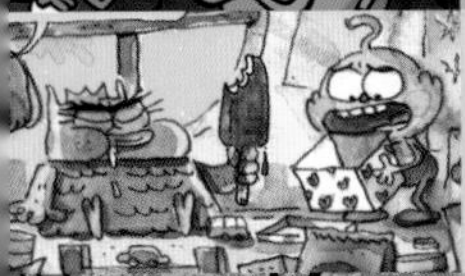

"COLD CASE"
Kevin Kramer – Writer
Saeid Zameniateni – Artist,
Colorist, Letterer

"SIBLING SPEAK"
Chris Savino – Creator,
Writer, Artist, Colorist, Letterer

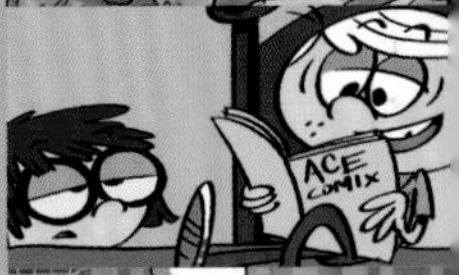
ACE
COMIX

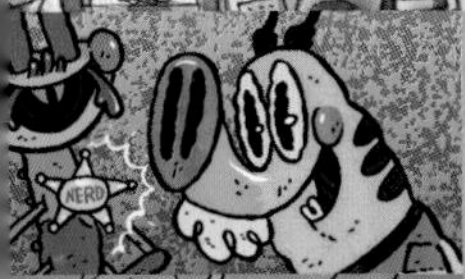
NERD

"TOUGHEST GUY IN HISTORY"
Eric Esquivel – Writer
David DeGrand – Artist
Laurie E. Smith – Colorist
Tom Orzechowski – Letterer

"DOUBLE AGENT DUCKS"
Eric Esquivel – Writer
Gary Fields – Artist
Laurie E. Smith – Colorist
Tom Orzechowski – Letterer

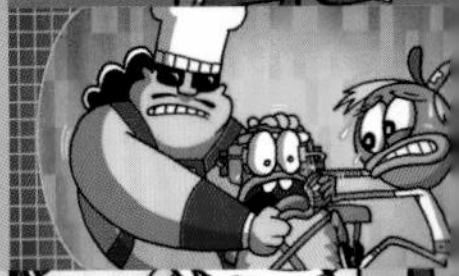

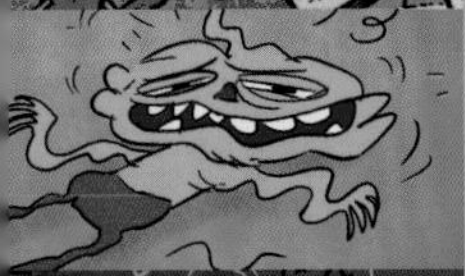

"FOO FACTS #93– PLAYING DEAD"
Carson Montgomery – Writer
Andreas Schuster – Artist, Letterer
Matteo Baldrighi – Colorist

"DEUCES WILD!"
Chris Savino – Creator, Writer, Artist, Letterer
Karla Sakas Shropshire – Writer
Jordan Rosato – Artist
Amanda Rynda – Colorist

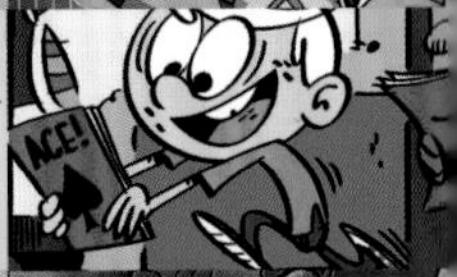
ACE!

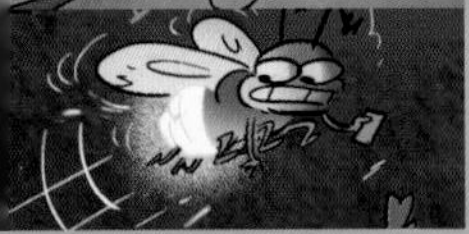

"OFFICER FREDD"
Jeffrey Trammell – Writer
Andreas Schuster – Artist, Letterer
Laurie E. Smith – Colorist

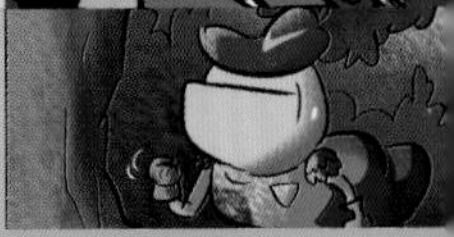

Breadwinners created by Gary "Doodles" DiRaffaele and Steve Borst
Harvey Beaks created by C.H. Greenblatt
Pig Goat Banana Cricket created by Johnny Ryan and Dave Cooper
Sanjay and Craig created by Jim Dirschberger, Jay Howell, and Andreas Trolf
The Loud House created by Chris Savino

Chris Savino, James Kaminski, Allison Strejlau, Andreas Schuster, David DeGrand and Laurie E. Smith – Cover Artists
James Salerno – Sr. Art Director/Nickelodeon
Dawn Guzzo – Design/Production
Rachel Pinnelas – Production Coordinator
Emelyne Tan, Melissa Kleynowski – Editorial Interns
Bethany Bryan,
Jeff Whitman – Editors
Joan Hilty – Comics Editor/Nickelodeon
Jim Salicrup
Editor-in-Chief
Chris Nelson and Carthin Henrichs – Special Thanks

ISBN: 978-1-62991-618-7 paperback edition
ISBN: 978-1-62991-619-4 hardcover edition

Papercutz books may be purchased for business or promotional use.
For information on bulk purchases please contact Macmillan Corporate and Premium Sales Department at (800) 221-7945 x5442.

Printed in China
January 2017 by Toppan Leefung Printing Limited

Distributed by Macmillan
First Printing

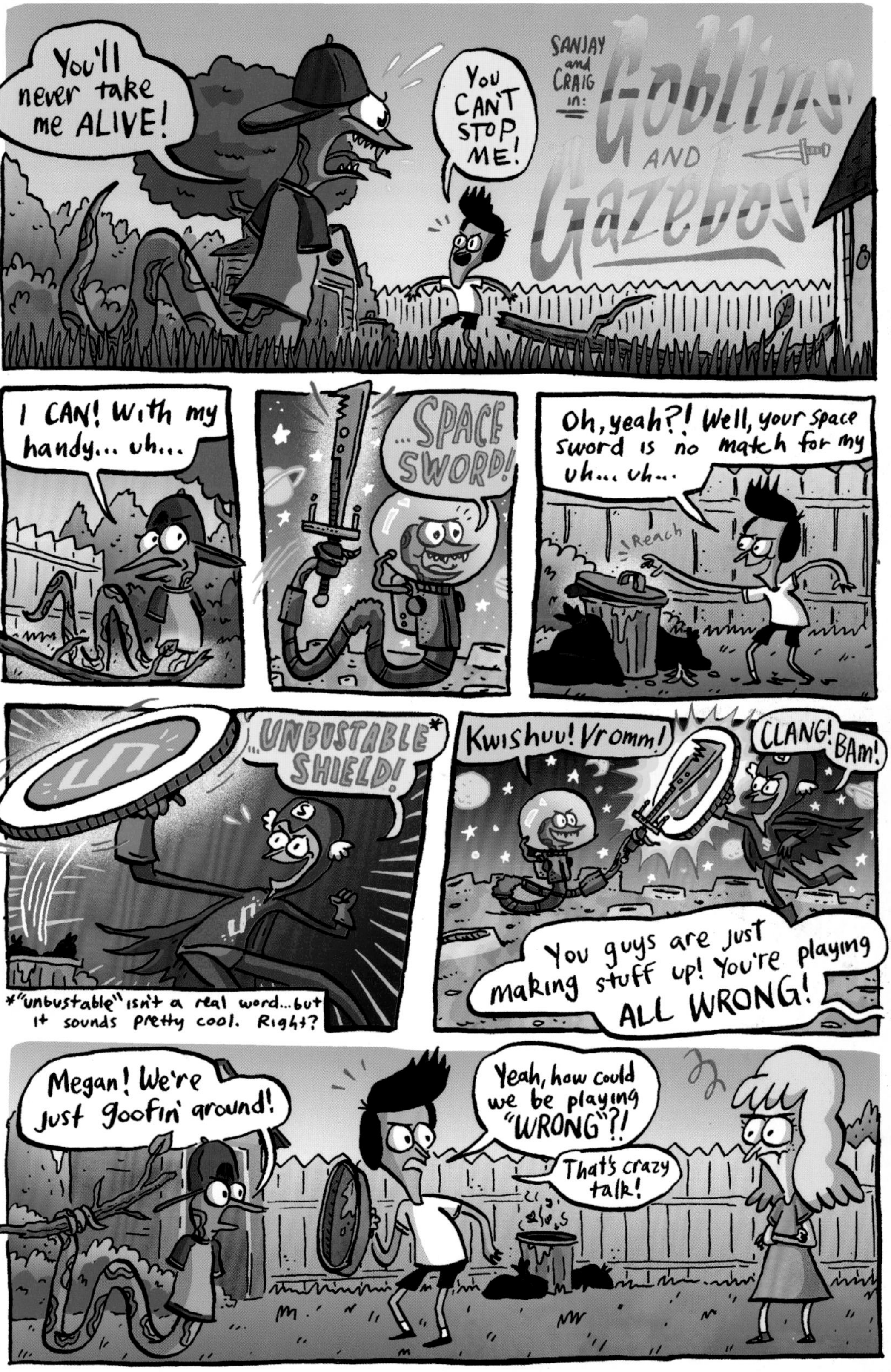

You'll never take me ALIVE!
You CAN'T STOP ME!
SANJAY and CRAIG in: Goblins and Gazebos
I CAN! With my handy... uh...
...SPACE SWORD!
Oh, yeah?! Well, your space sword is no match for my uh... uh...
Reach
...UNBUSTABLE* SHIELD!
*"unbustable" isn't a real word...but it sounds pretty cool. Right?
Kwishuu! Vromm!
CLANG! BAM!
You guys are just making stuff up! You're playing ALL WRONG!
Megan! We're just goofin' around!
Yeah, how could we be playing "WRONG"?!
That's crazy talk!

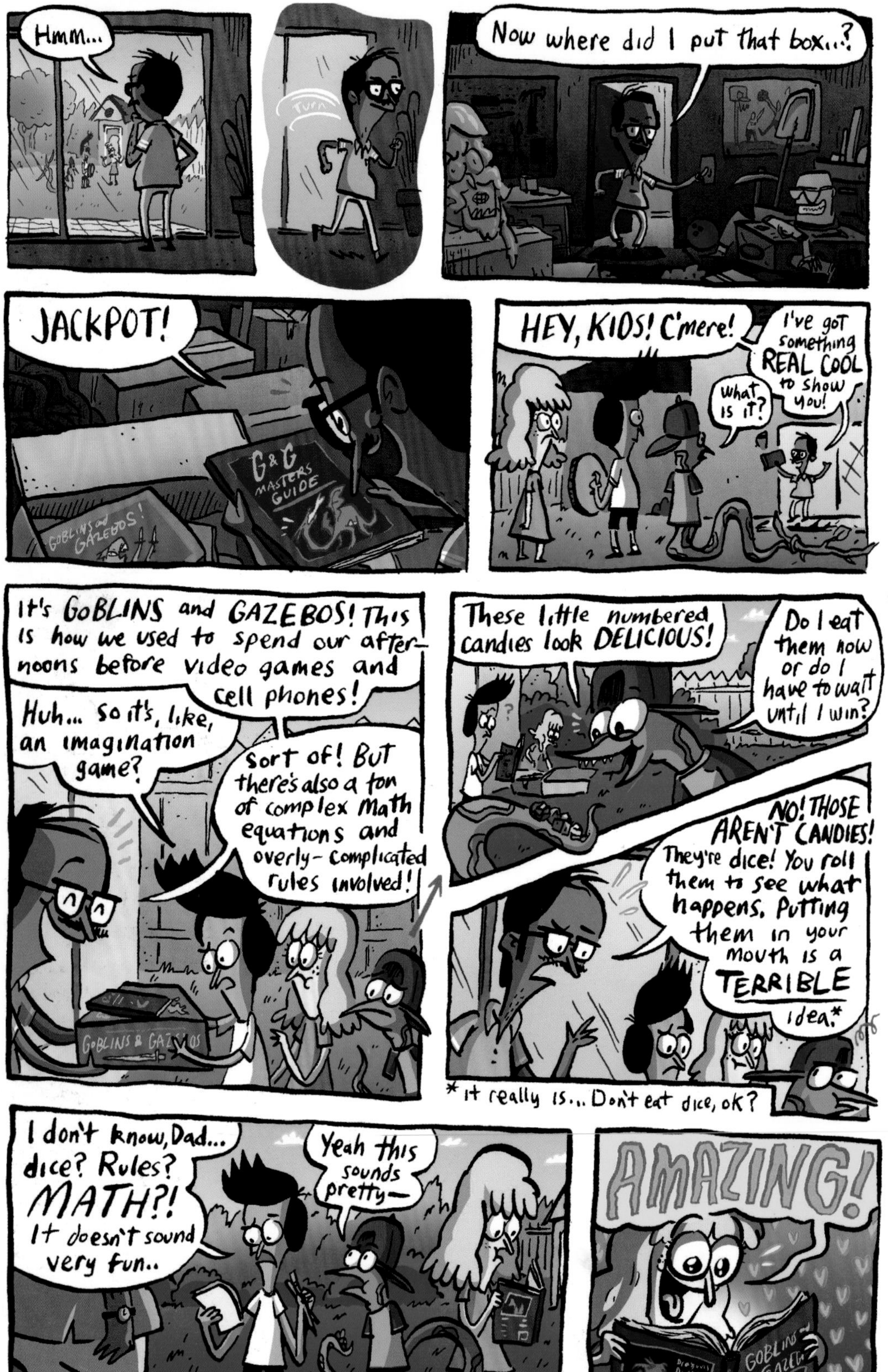
Hmm...
TURN
Now where did I put that box...?
JACKPOT!
G & G MASTERS GUIDE
GOBLINS and GAZEBOS!
HEY, KIDS! C'mere!
I've got something REAL COOL to show you!
What is it?
It's GOBLINS and GAZEBOS! This is how we used to spend our after-noons before video games and cell phones!
Huh... so it's, like, an imagination game?
Sort of! But there's also a ton of complex Math equations and overly-complicated rules involved!
GOBLINS & GAZEBOS
These little numbered candies look DELICIOUS!
Do I eat them now or do I have to wait until I win?
NO! THOSE AREN'T CANDIES!
They're dice! You roll them to see what happens. Putting them in your mouth is a TERRIBLE idea.*
* it really is... Don't eat dice, ok?
I don't know, Dad... dice? Rules? MATH?! It doesn't sound very fun..
Yeah this sounds pretty—
AMAZING!
GOBLINS & GAZEBOS

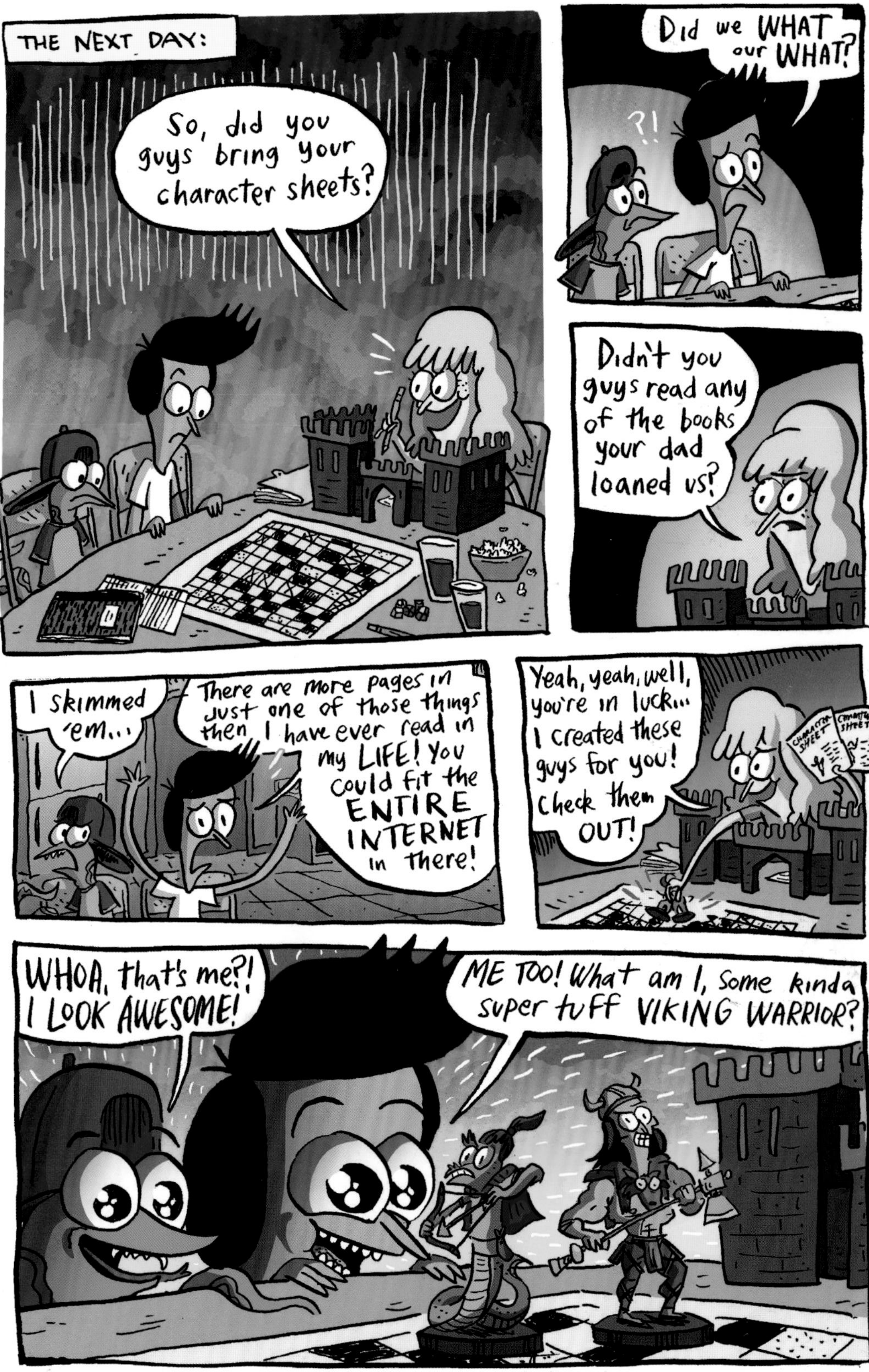
THE NEXT DAY:
So, did you guys bring your character sheets?
Did we WHAT our WHAT?
?!
Didn't you guys read any of the books your dad loaned us?
I skimmed 'em...
There are more pages in just one of those things then I have ever read in my LIFE! You could fit the ENTIRE INTERNET in there!
Yeah, yeah, well, you're in luck... I created these guys for you! Check them OUT!
CHARACTER SHEET
CHARACTER SHEET
WHOA, that's me?! I LOOK AWESOME!
ME TOO! What am I, some kinda super tuff VIKING WARRIOR?

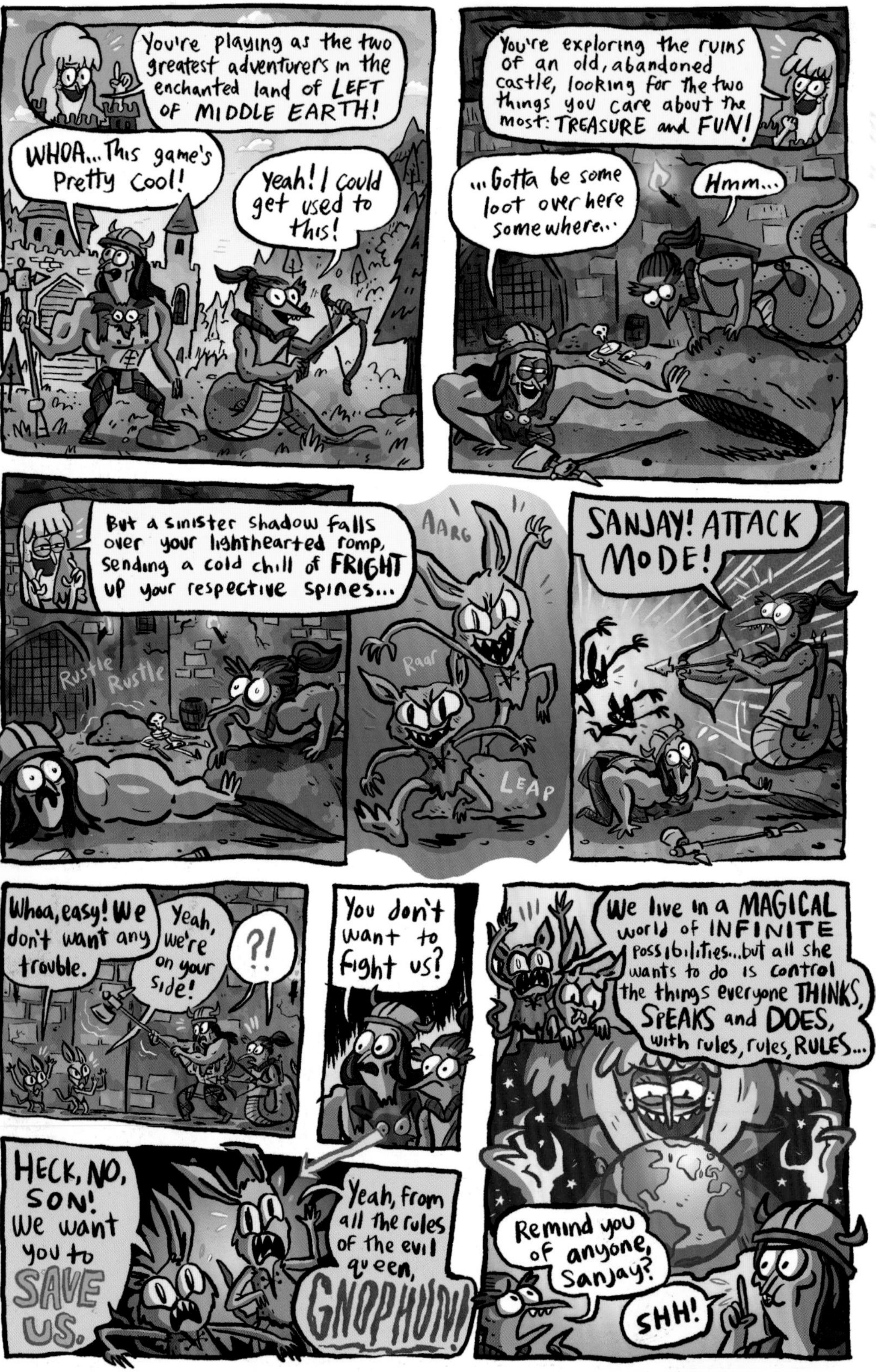
You're playing as the two greatest adventurers in the enchanted land of LEFT OF MIDDLE EARTH!
WHOA... This game's pretty cool!
Yeah! I could get used to this!
You're exploring the ruins of an old, abandoned castle, looking for the two things you care about the most: TREASURE and FUN!
...Gotta be some loot over here somewhere...
Hmm...
But a sinister shadow falls over your lighthearted romp, sending a cold chill of FRIGHT up your respective spines...
Rustle Rustle
AARG
Raar
LEAP
SANJAY! ATTACK MODE!
Whoa, easy! We don't want any trouble.
Yeah, we're on your side!
?!
You don't want to fight us?
HECK, NO, SON! We want you to SAVE US.
Yeah, from all the rules of the evil queen, GNOPHUN!
We live in a MAGICAL world of INFINITE possibilities...but all she wants to do is control the things everyone THINKS, SPEAKS and DOES, with rules, rules, RULES...
Remind you of anyone, Sanjay?
SHH!

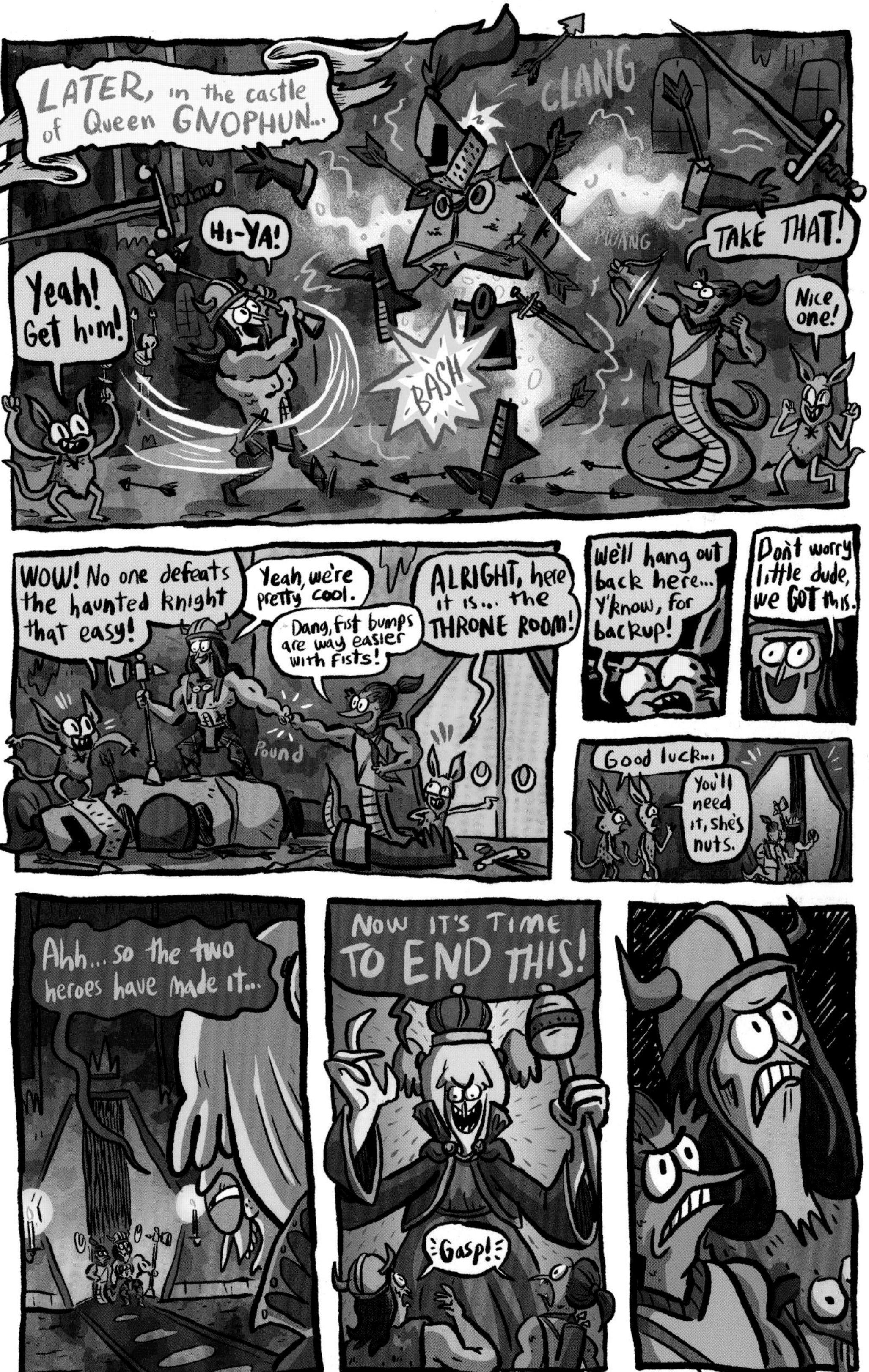
LATER, in the castle of Queen GNOPHUN...
CLANG
HI-YA!
Yeah! Get him!
PWANG
TAKE THAT!
Nice one!
BASH
WOW! No one defeats the haunted knight that easy!
Yeah, we're pretty cool.
Dang, fist bumps are way easier with fists!
Pound
ALRIGHT, here it is... the THRONE ROOM!
We'll hang out back here... Y'know, for backup!
Don't worry little dude, we GOT this.
Good luck...
You'll need it, she's nuts.
Ahh... so the two heroes have made it...
NOW IT'S TIME TO END THIS!
Gasp!

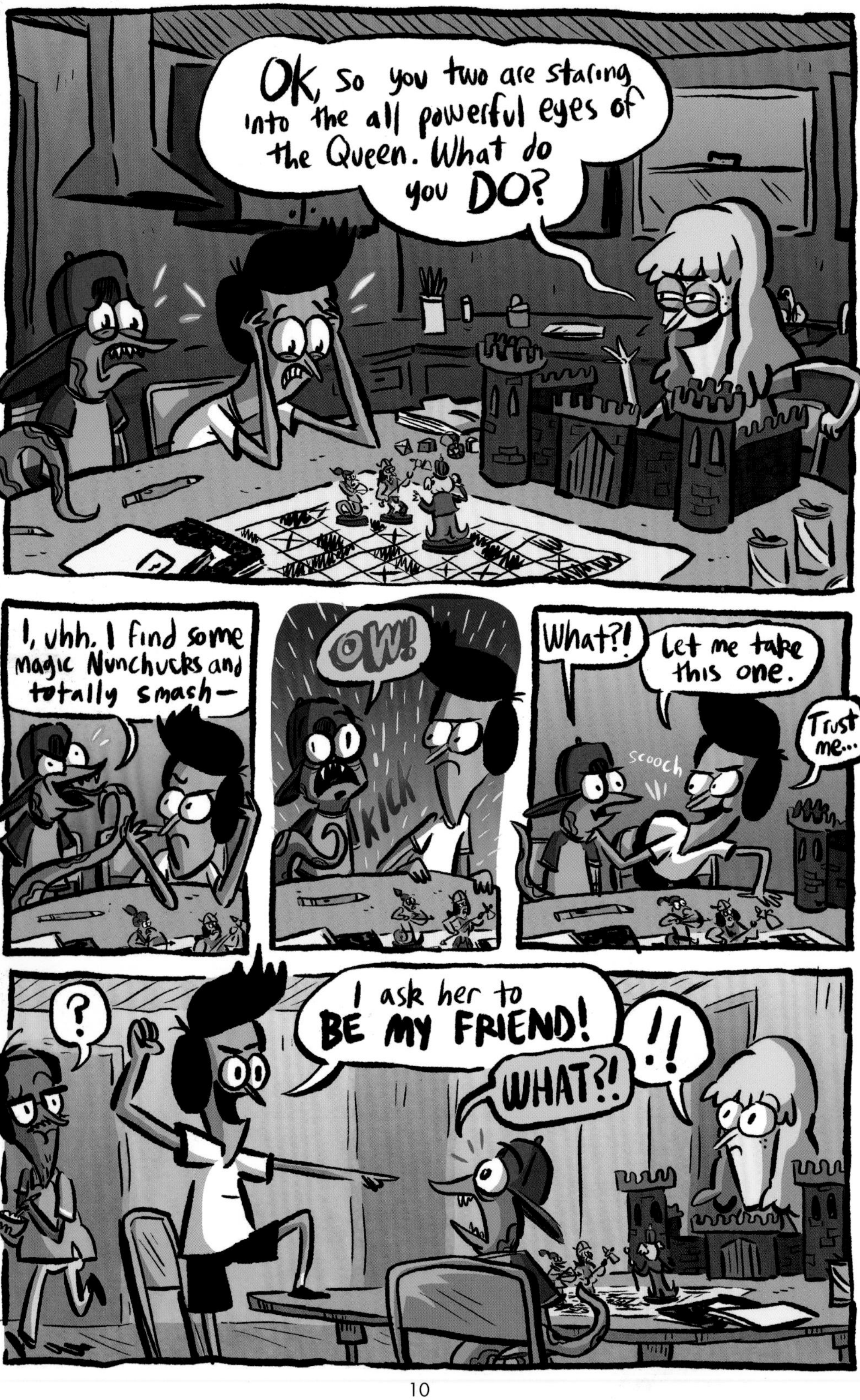
OK, so you two are staring into the all powerful eyes of the Queen. What do you DO?
I, uhh. I find some magic Nunchucks and totally smash—
OW!
KICK
What?!
Let me take this one.
scooch
Trust me...
?
I ask her to BE MY FRIEND!
WHAT?!
!!

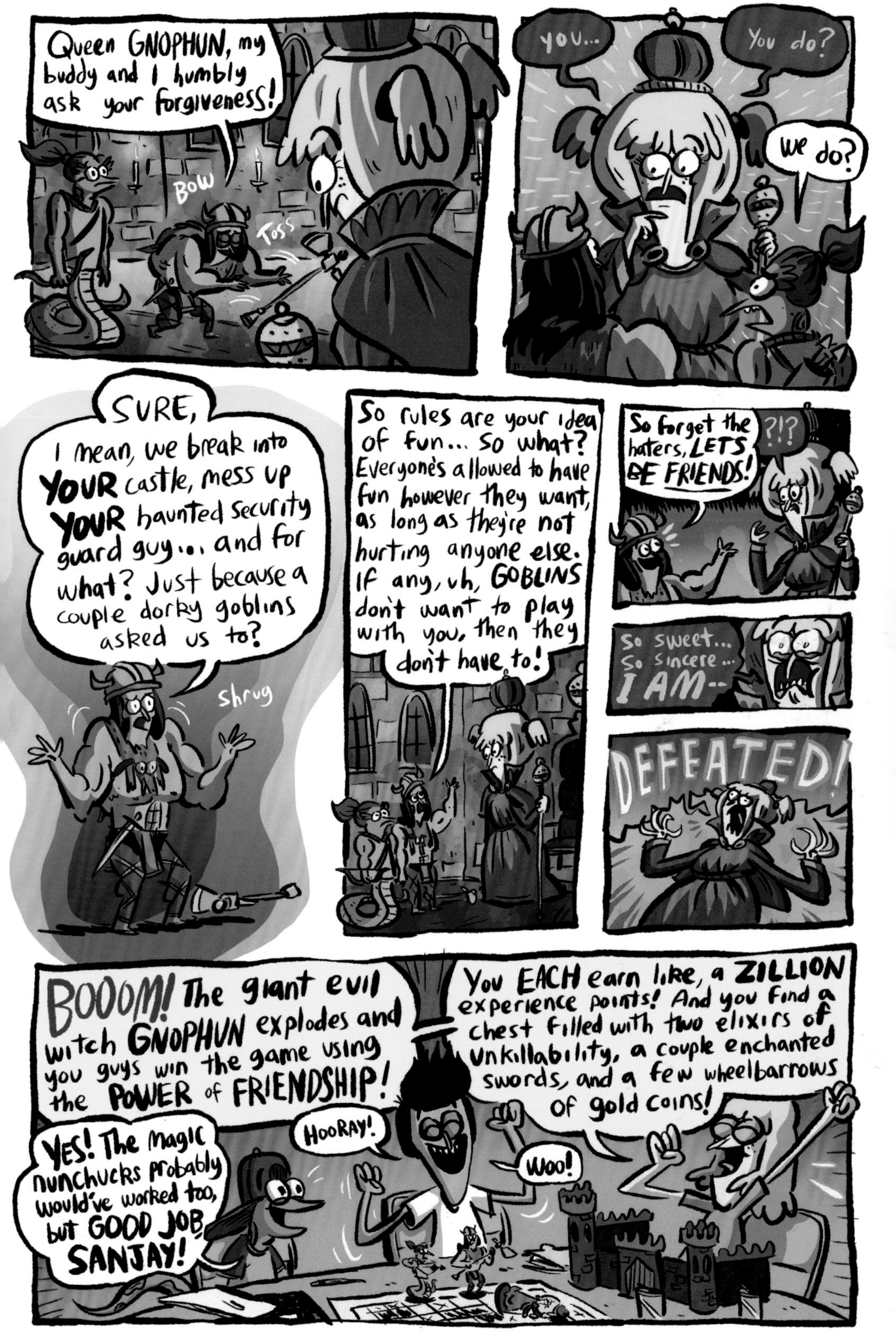
Queen GNOPHUN, my buddy and I humbly ask your forgiveness!
BOW
TOSS
YOU...
You do?
We do?
SURE, I mean, we break into YOUR castle, mess up YOUR haunted security guard guy... and for what? Just because a couple dorky goblins asked us to?
shrug
So rules are your idea of fun... So what? Everyone's allowed to have fun however they want, as long as they're not hurting anyone else. If any, uh, GOBLINS don't want to play with you, then they don't have to!
So forget the haters, LETS BE FRIENDS!
?!?
So sweet... So sincere... I AM--
DEFEATED!
BOOOM! The giant evil witch GNOPHUN explodes and you guys win the game using the POWER of FRIENDSHIP!
You EACH earn like, a ZILLION experience points! And you find a chest filled with two elixirs of unkillability, a couple enchanted swords, and a few wheelbarrows of gold coins!
YES! The magic nunchucks probably would've worked too, but GOOD JOB SANJAY!
HOORAY!
WOO!

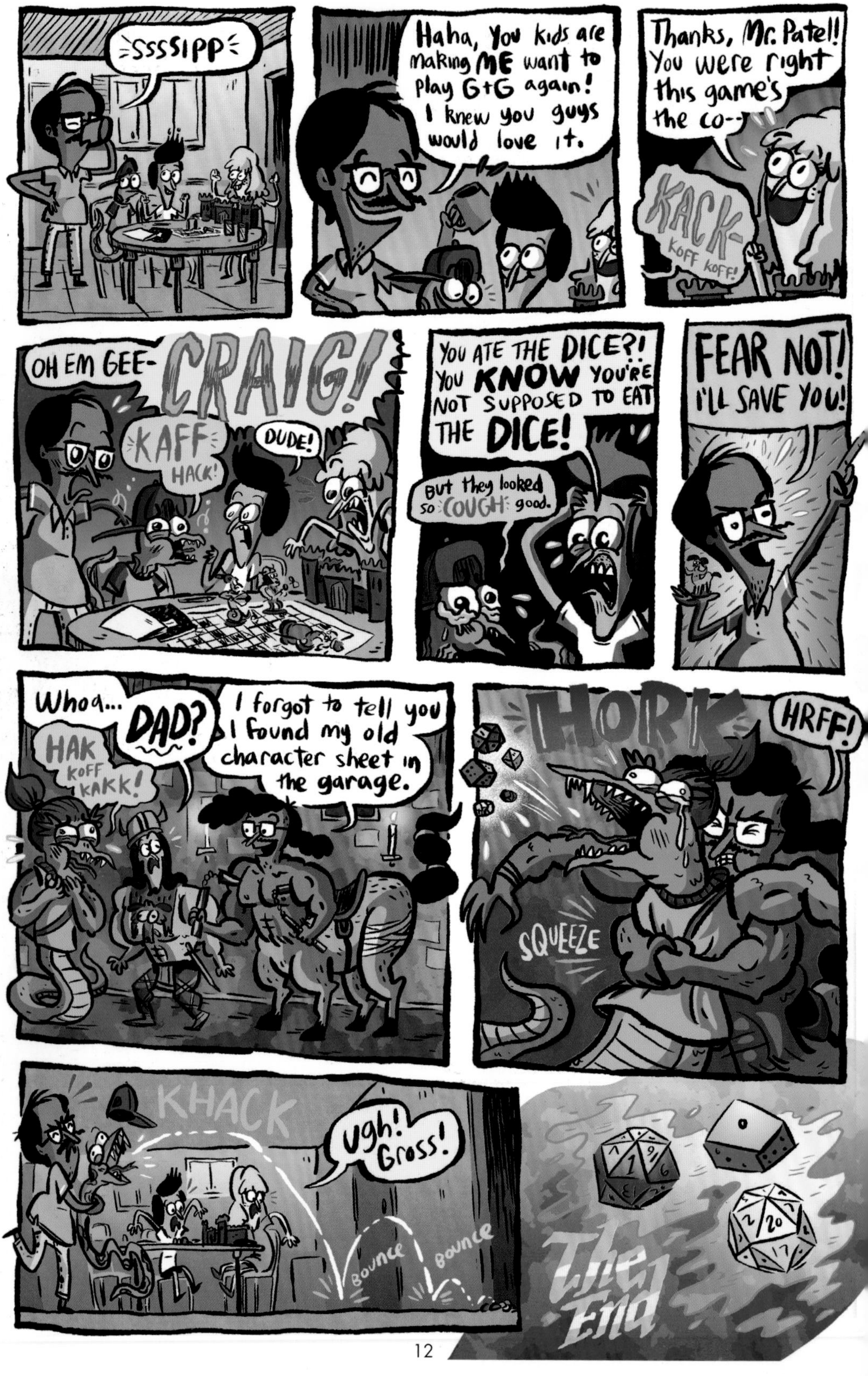
SSSSIPP
Haha, you kids are making ME want to play G+G again! I knew you guys would love it.
Thanks, Mr. Patel! You were right this game's the co--
KACK-
KOFF KOFF!
OH EM GEE-
CRAIG!
KAFF
HACK!
DUDE!
YOU ATE THE DICE?! YOU KNOW YOU'RE NOT SUPPOSED TO EAT THE DICE!
But they looked so COUGH good.
FEAR NOT! I'LL SAVE YOU!
Whoa... DAD?
HAK KOFF KAKK!
I forgot to tell you I found my old character sheet in the garage.
HORK
HRFF!
SQUEEZE
KHACK
Ugh! Gross!
BOUNCE
BOUNCE
The End

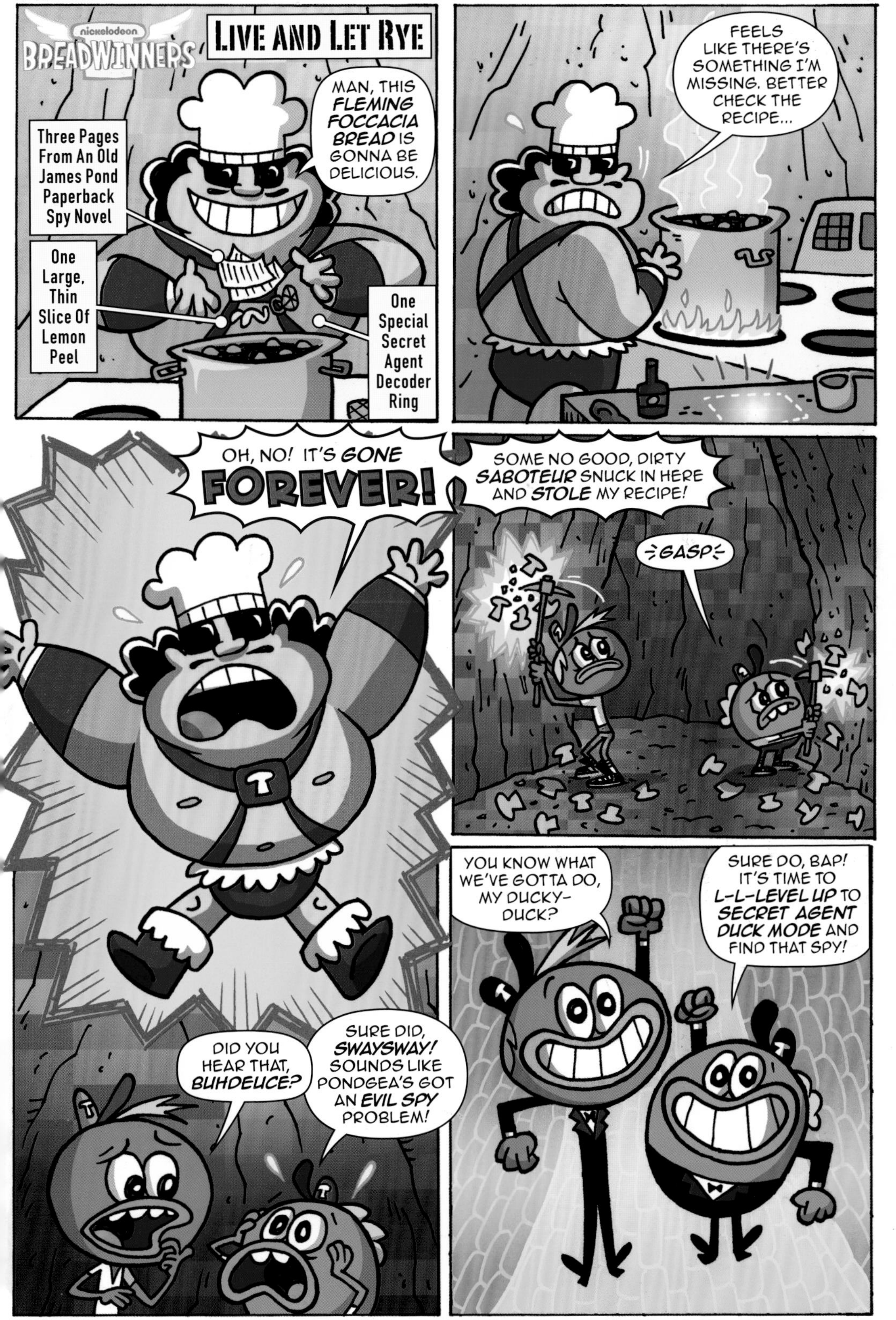
nickelodeon
BREADWINNERS
LIVE AND LET RYE
MAN, THIS FLEMING FOCCACIA BREAD IS GONNA BE DELICIOUS.
Three Pages From An Old James Pond Paperback Spy Novel
One Large, Thin Slice Of Lemon Peel
One Special Secret Agent Decoder Ring
FEELS LIKE THERE'S SOMETHING I'M MISSING. BETTER CHECK THE RECIPE...
OH, NO! IT'S GONE FOREVER!
SOME NO GOOD, DIRTY SABOTEUR SNUCK IN HERE AND STOLE MY RECIPE!
GASP
DID YOU HEAR THAT, BUHDEUCE?
SURE DID, SWAYSWAY! SOUNDS LIKE PONDGEA'S GOT AN EVIL SPY PROBLEM!
YOU KNOW WHAT WE'VE GOTTA DO, MY DUCKY-DUCK?
SURE DO, BAP! IT'S TIME TO L-L-LEVEL UP TO SECRET AGENT DUCK MODE AND FIND THAT SPY!

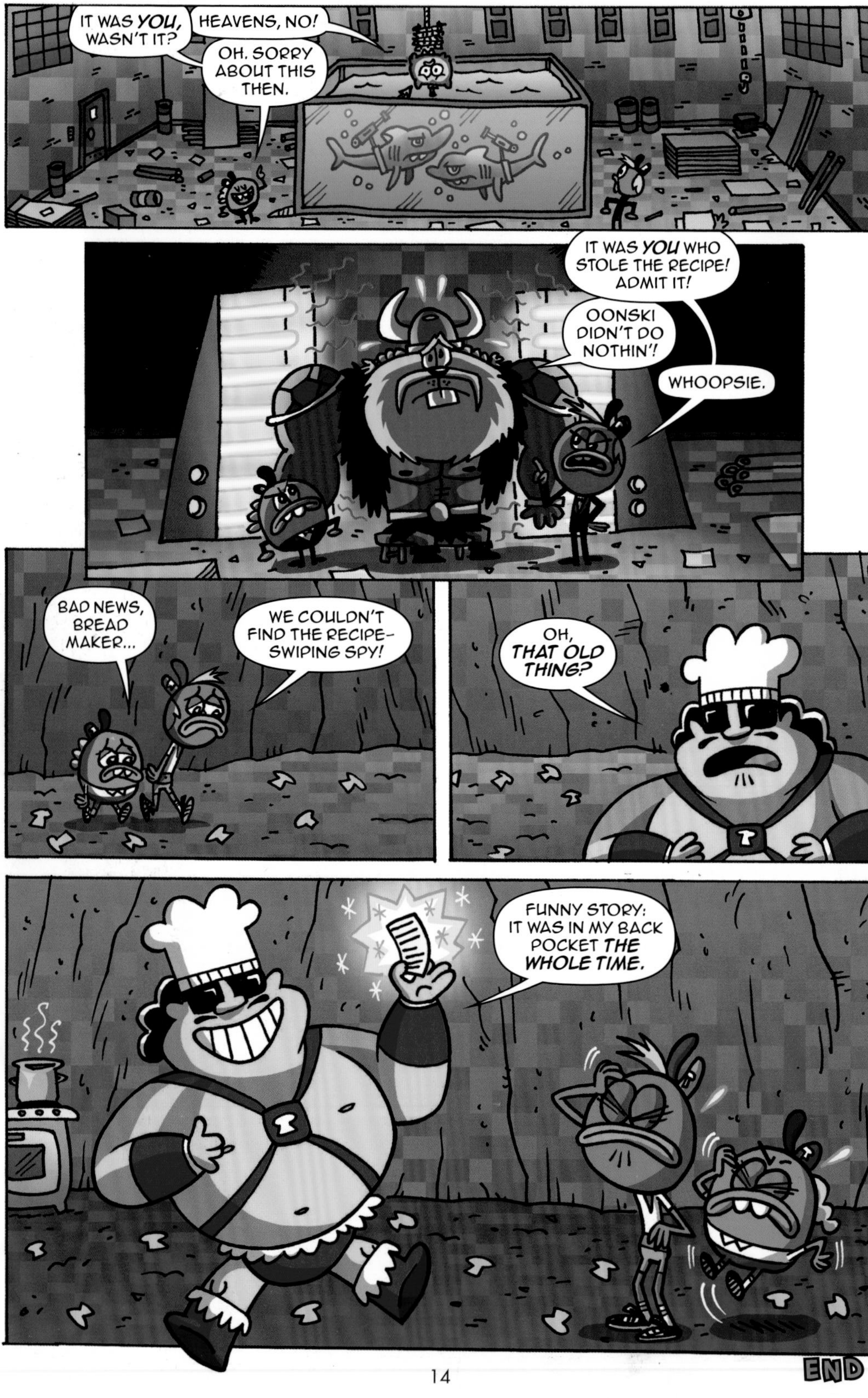
IT WAS YOU, WASN'T IT?
HEAVENS, NO!
OH. SORRY ABOUT THIS THEN.
IT WAS YOU WHO STOLE THE RECIPE! ADMIT IT!
OONSKI DIDN'T DO NOTHIN'!
WHOOPSIE.
BAD NEWS, BREAD MAKER...
WE COULDN'T FIND THE RECIPE-SWIPING SPY!
OH, THAT OLD THING?
FUNNY STORY: IT WAS IN MY BACK POCKET THE WHOLE TIME.
END

COLD CASE

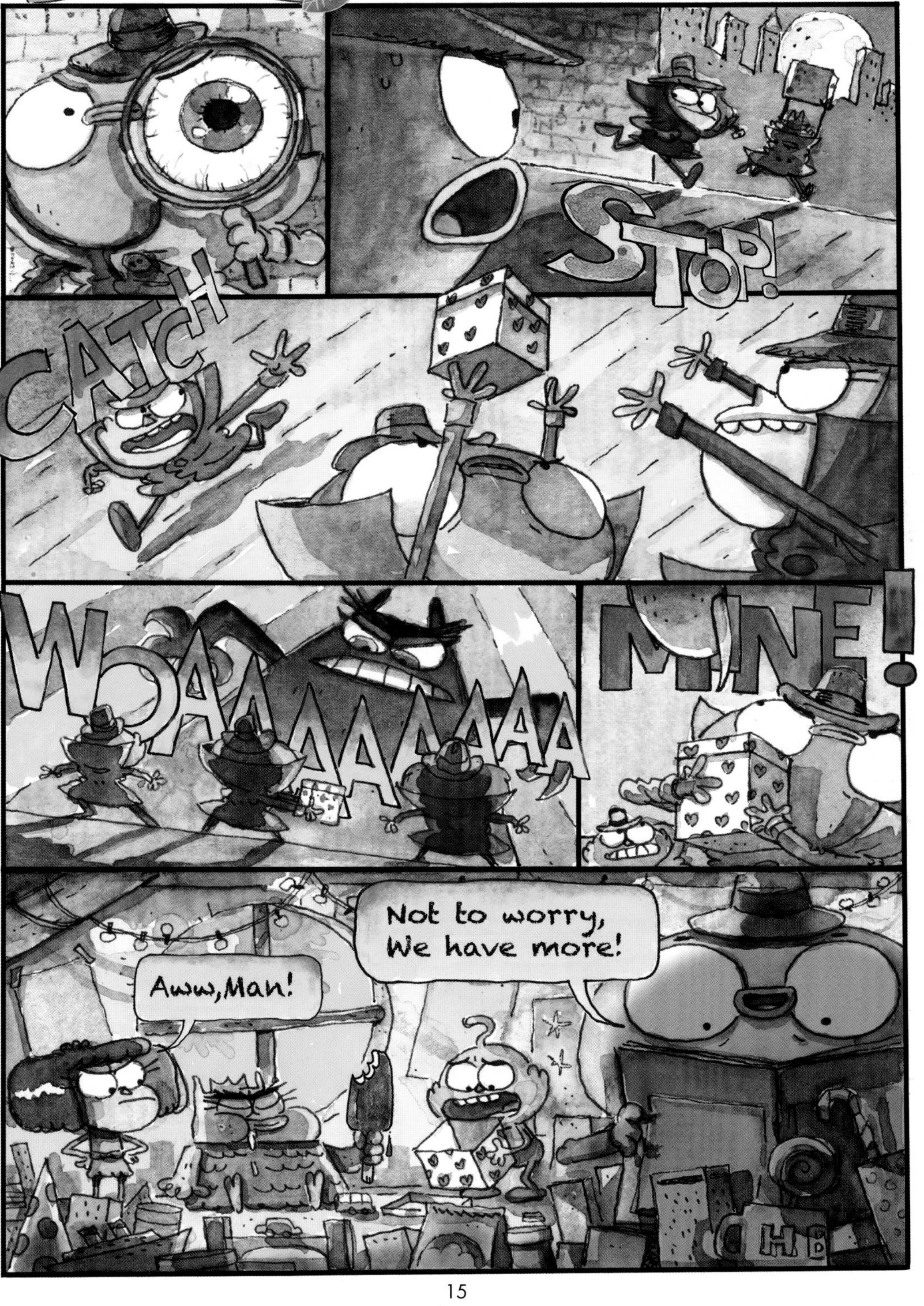
STOP!
CATCH
WOAAAAAAAA
MINE!
Aww, Man!
Not to worry,
We have more!

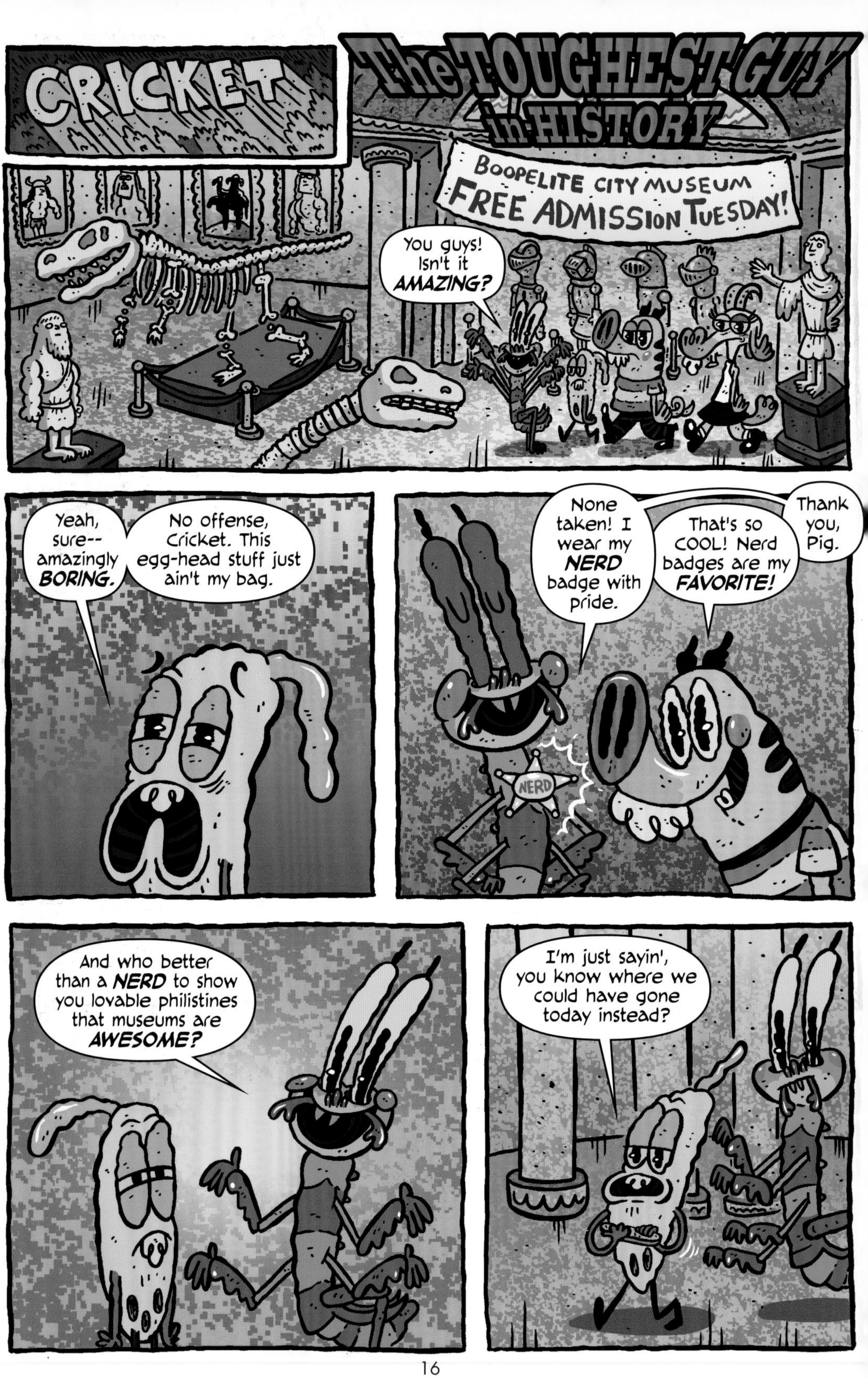
CRICKET
The TOUGHEST GUY in HISTORY
BOOPELITE CITY MUSEUM
FREE ADMISSION TUESDAY!
You guys! Isn't it AMAZING?
Yeah, sure--amazingly BORING.
No offense, Cricket. This egg-head stuff just ain't my bag.
None taken! I wear my NERD badge with pride.
That's so COOL! Nerd badges are my FAVORITE!
Thank you, Pig.
NERD
And who better than a NERD to show you lovable philistines that museums are AWESOME?
I'm just sayin', you know where we could have gone today instead?

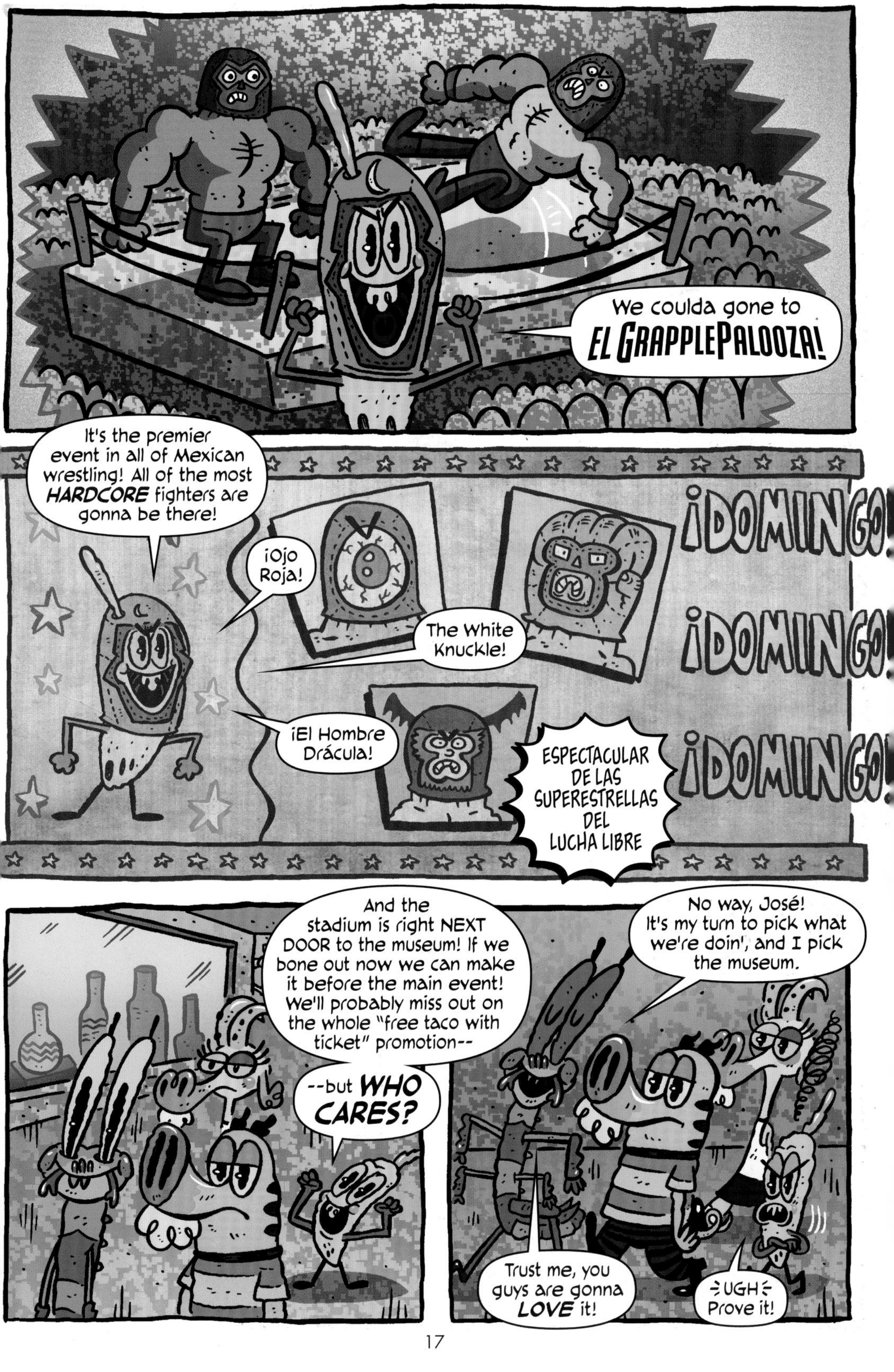
We coulda gone to EL GRAPPLEPALOOZA!
It's the premier event in all of Mexican wrestling! All of the most HARDCORE fighters are gonna be there!
¡Ojo Roja!
The White Knuckle!
¡El Hombre Drácula!
ESPECTACULAR DE LAS SUPERESTRELLAS DEL LUCHA LIBRE
¡DOMINGO!
¡DOMINGO!
¡DOMINGO!
And the stadium is right NEXT DOOR to the museum! If we bone out now we can make it before the main event! We'll probably miss out on the whole "free taco with ticket" promotion--
--but WHO CARES?
No way, José! It's my turn to pick what we're doin', and I pick the museum.
Trust me, you guys are gonna LOVE it!
UGH Prove it!

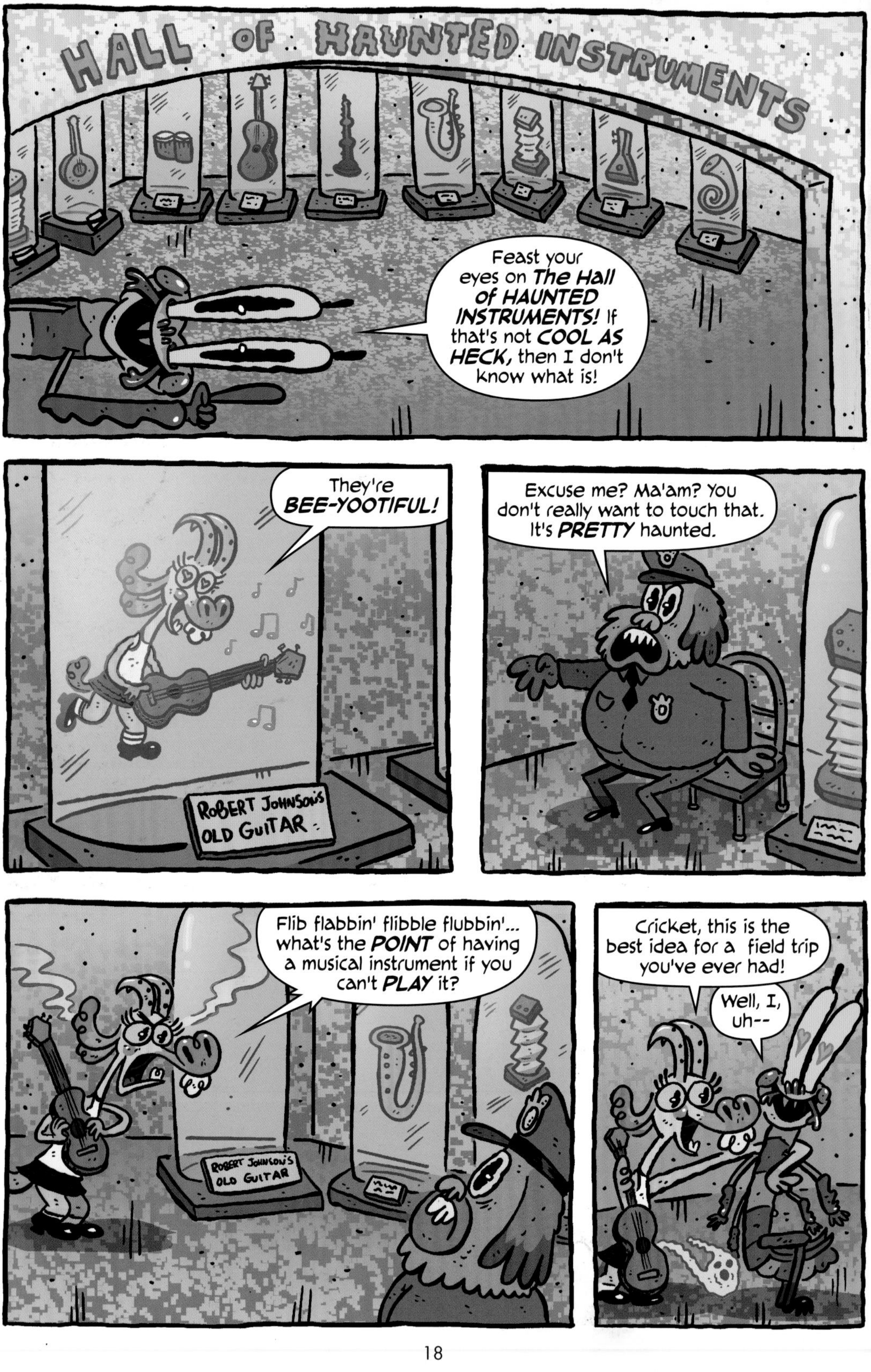
HALL of HAUNTED INSTRUMENTS
Feast your eyes on The Hall of HAUNTED INSTRUMENTS! If that's not COOL AS HECK, then I don't know what is!
They're BEE-YOOTIFUL!
ROBERT JOHNSON'S OLD GUITAR
Excuse me? Ma'am? You don't really want to touch that. It's PRETTY haunted.
Flib flabbin' flibble flubbin'... what's the POINT of having a musical instrument if you can't PLAY it?
ROBERT JOHNSON'S OLD GUITAR
Cricket, this is the best idea for a field trip you've ever had!
Well, I, uh--

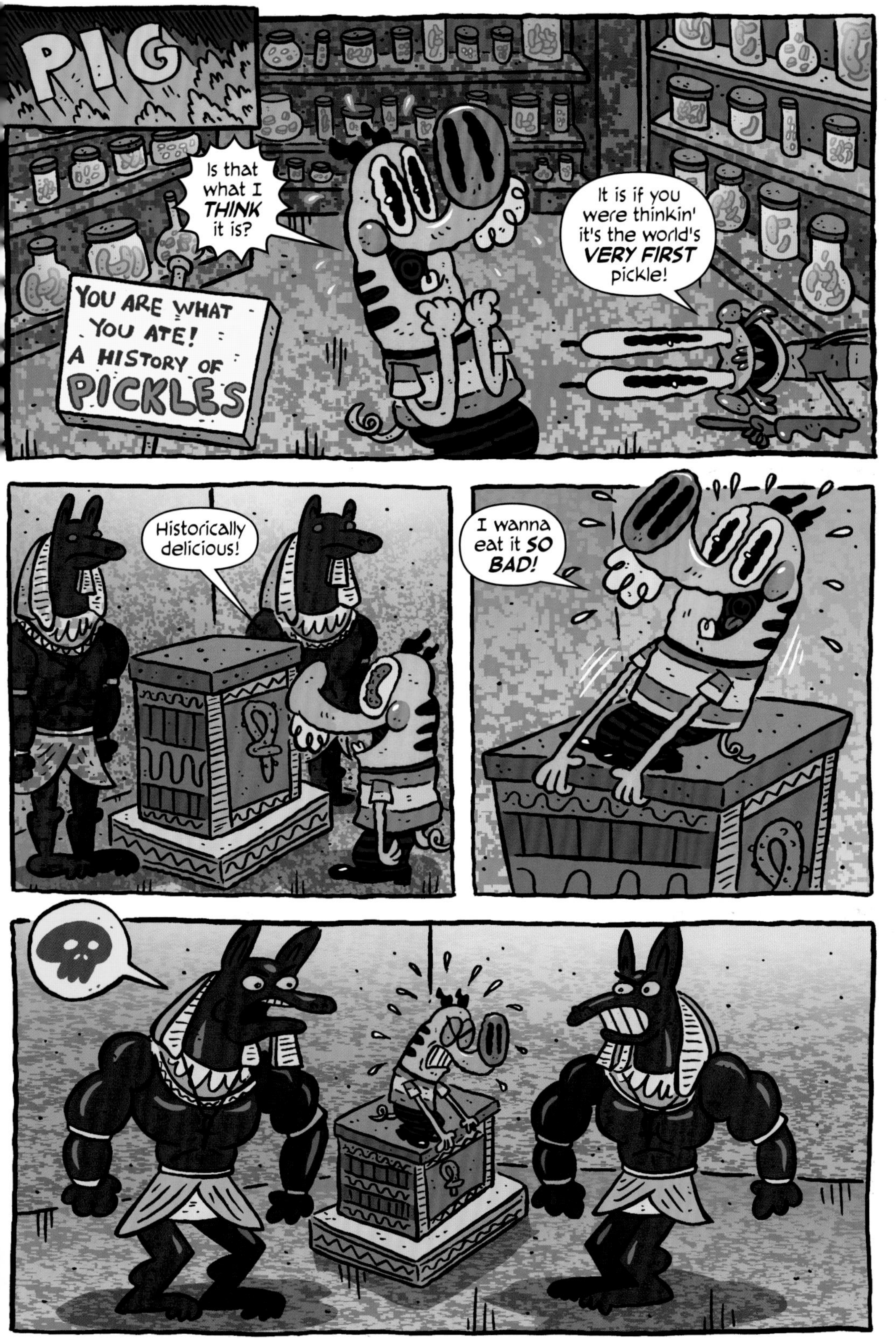
PIG
Is that what I *THINK* it is?
YOU ARE WHAT YOU ATE! A HISTORY OF PICKLES
It is if you were thinkin' it's the world's *VERY FIRST* pickle!
Historically delicious!
I wanna eat it *SO BAD!*

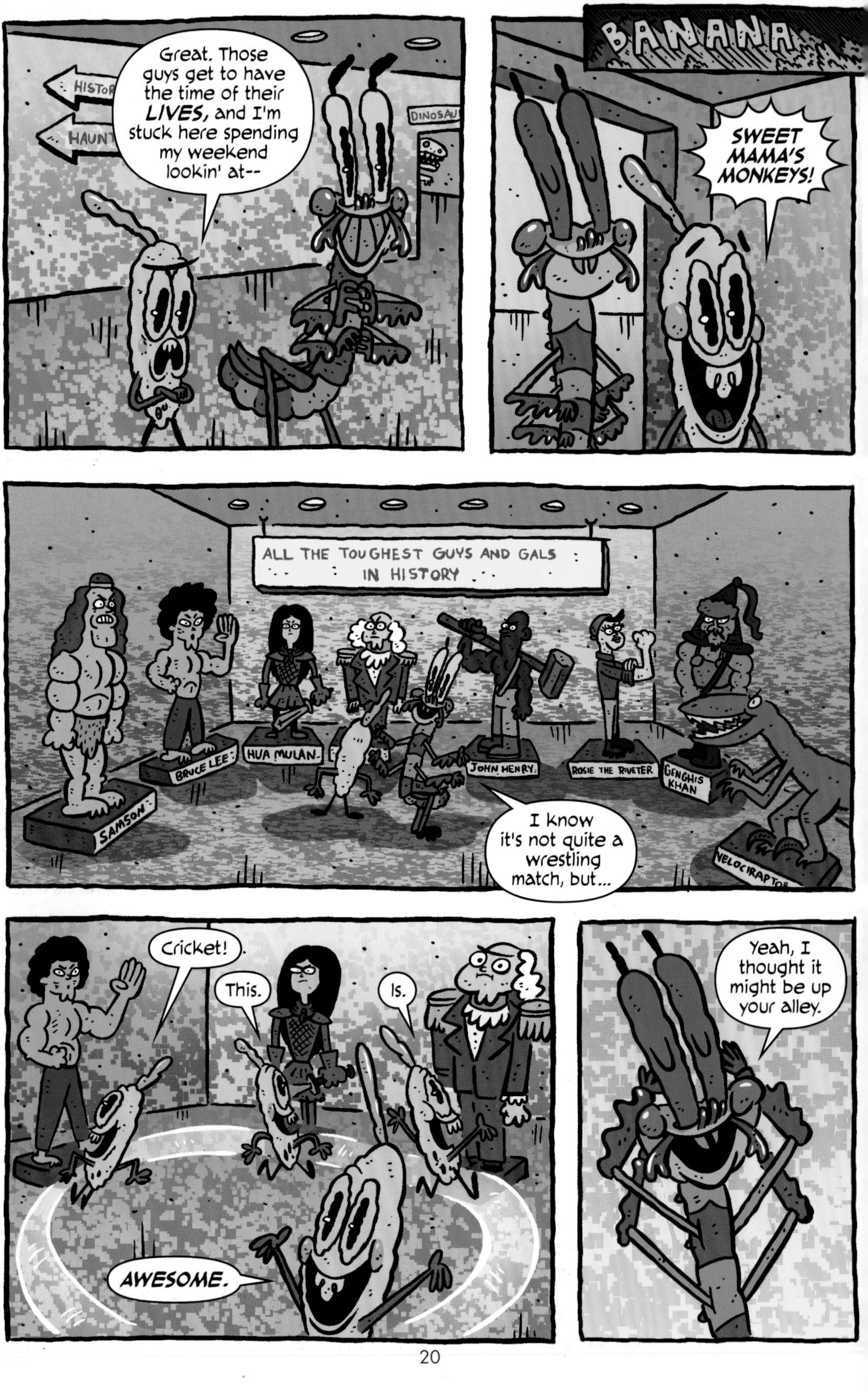
HISTOR
HAUNT
DINOSAU
Great. Those guys get to have the time of their LIVES, and I'm stuck here spending my weekend lookin' at--
BANANA
SWEET MAMA'S MONKEYS!
ALL THE TOUGHEST GUYS AND GALS IN HISTORY
SAMSON
BRUCE LEE
HUA MULAN
JOHN HENRY
ROSIE THE RIVETER
GENGHIS KHAN
VELOCIRAPTOR
I know it's not quite a wrestling match, but...
Cricket!
This.
Is.
AWESOME.
Yeah, I thought it might be up your alley.

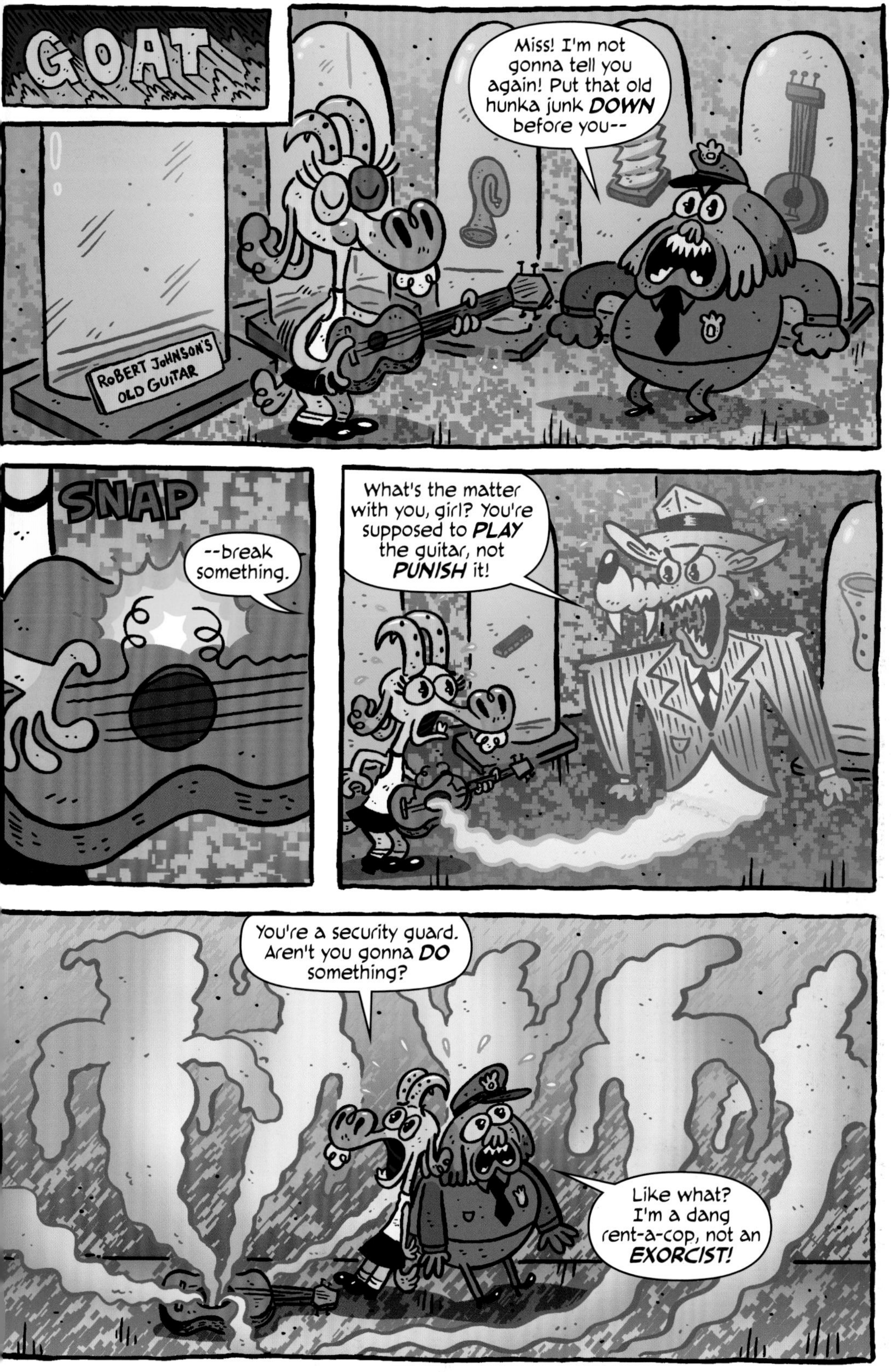
GOAT
Miss! I'm not gonna tell you again! Put that old hunka junk DOWN before you--
ROBERT JOHNSON'S OLD GUITAR
SNAP
--break something.
What's the matter with you, girl? You're supposed to PLAY the guitar, not PUNISH it!
You're a security guard. Aren't you gonna DO something?
Like what? I'm a dang rent-a-cop, not an EXORCIST!

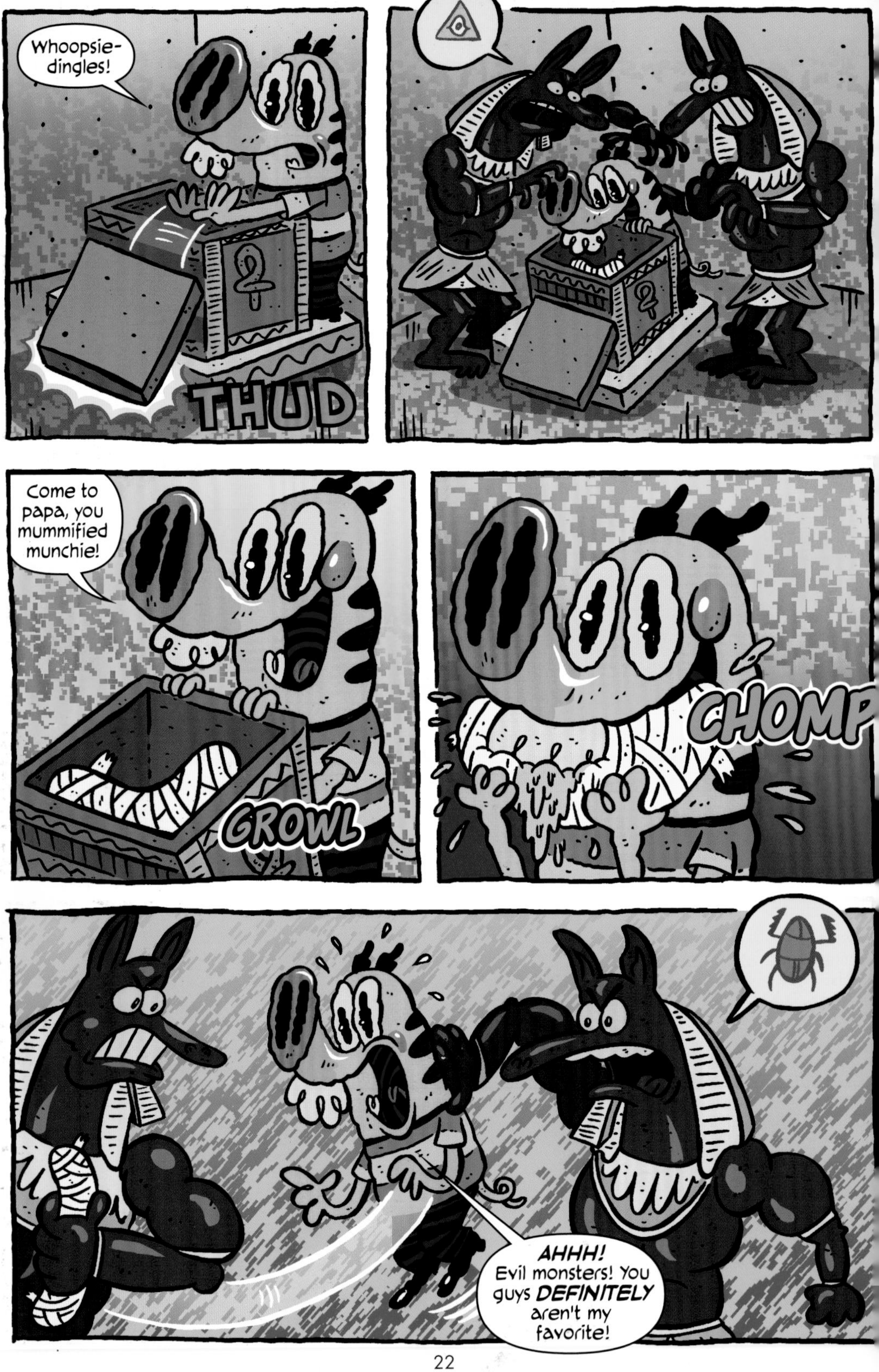
Whoopsie-dingles!
THUD
Come to papa, you mummified munchie!
GROWL
CHOMP
AHHH! Evil monsters! You guys DEFINITELY aren't my favorite!

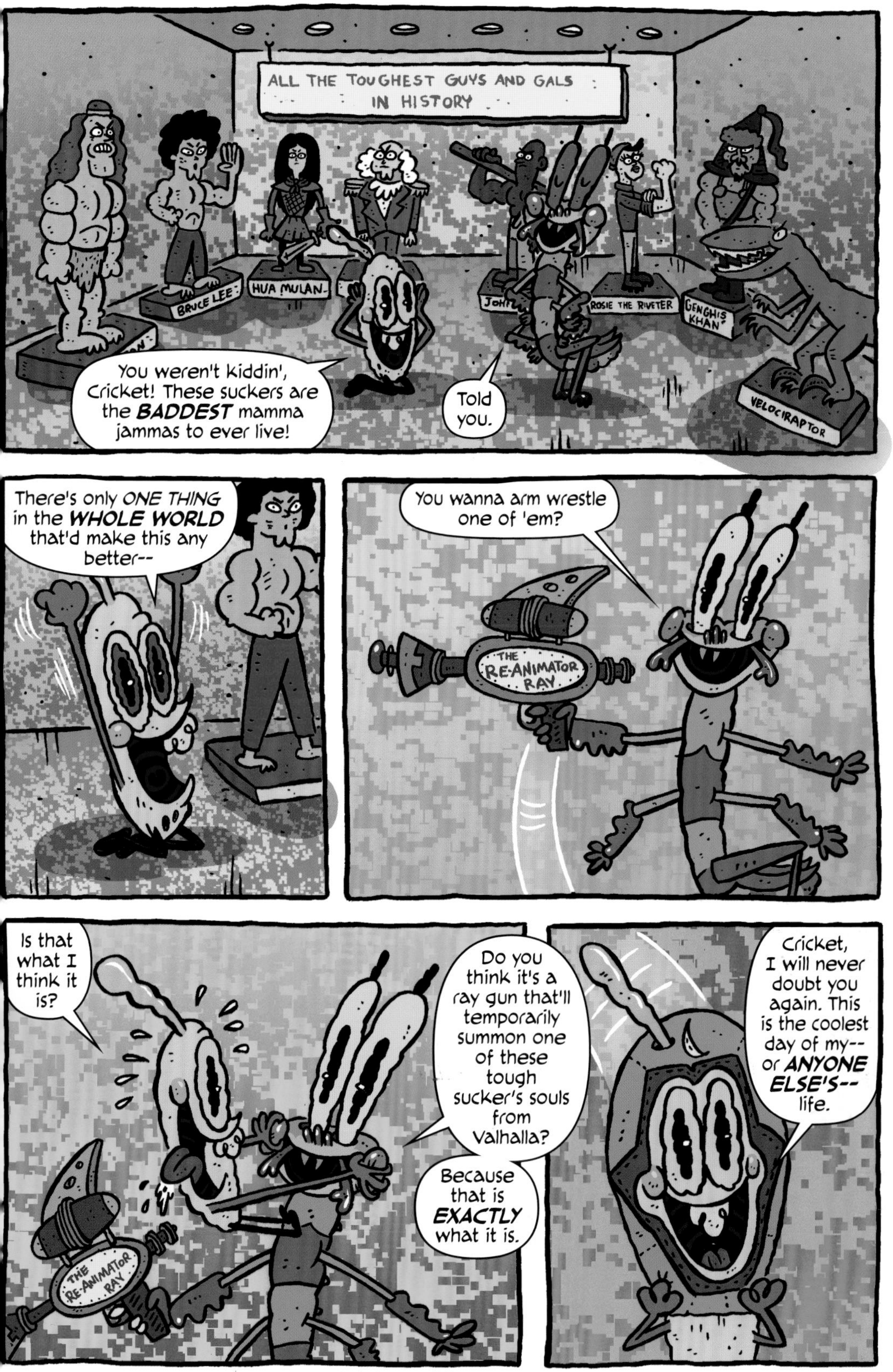
ALL THE TOUGHEST GUYS AND GALS IN HISTORY
BRUCE LEE
HUA MULAN
ROSIE THE RIVETER
GENGHIS KHAN
VELOCIRAPTOR
You weren't kiddin', Cricket! These suckers are the **BADDEST** mamma jammas to ever live!
Told you.
There's only *ONE THING* in the ***WHOLE WORLD*** that'd make this any better--
You wanna arm wrestle one of 'em?
THE RE-ANIMATOR RAY
Is that what I think it is?
Do you think it's a ray gun that'll temporarily summon one of these tough sucker's souls from Valhalla?
Because that is ***EXACTLY*** what it is.
THE RE-ANIMATOR RAY
Cricket, I will never doubt you again. This is the coolest day of my-- or ***ANYONE ELSE'S--*** life.

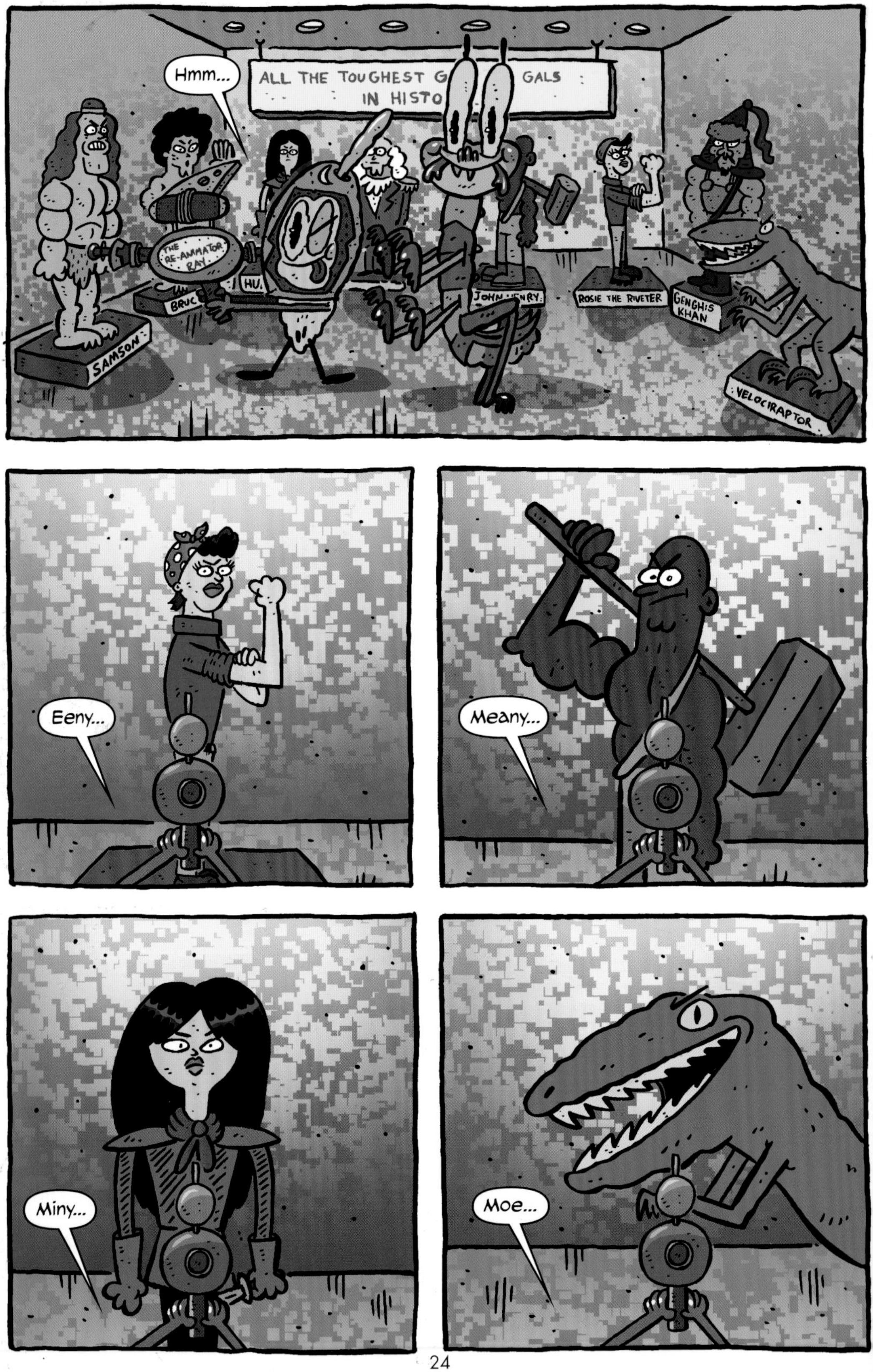
Hmm...
ALL THE TOUGHEST G GALS
IN HISTO
THE RE-ANIMATOR RAY
SAMSON
BRUC
HU
JOHN HENRY
ROSIE THE RIVETER
GENGHIS KHAN
VELOCIRAPTOR
Eeny...
Meany...
Miny...
Moe...

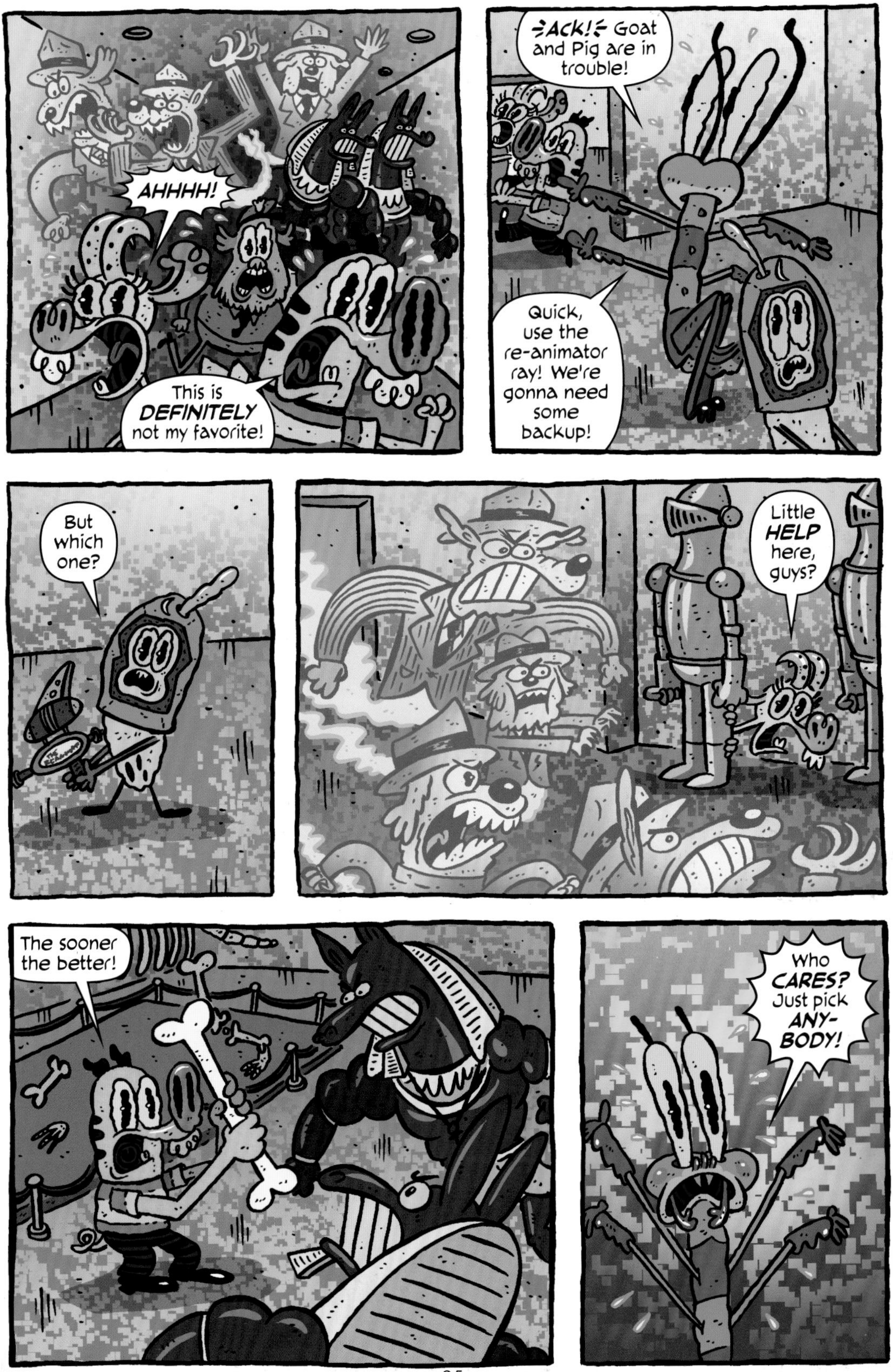
AHHHH!
This is DEFINITELY not my favorite!
ACK! Goat and Pig are in trouble!
Quick, use the re-animator ray! We're gonna need some backup!
But which one?
Little HELP here, guys?
The sooner the better!
Who CARES? Just pick ANY-BODY!

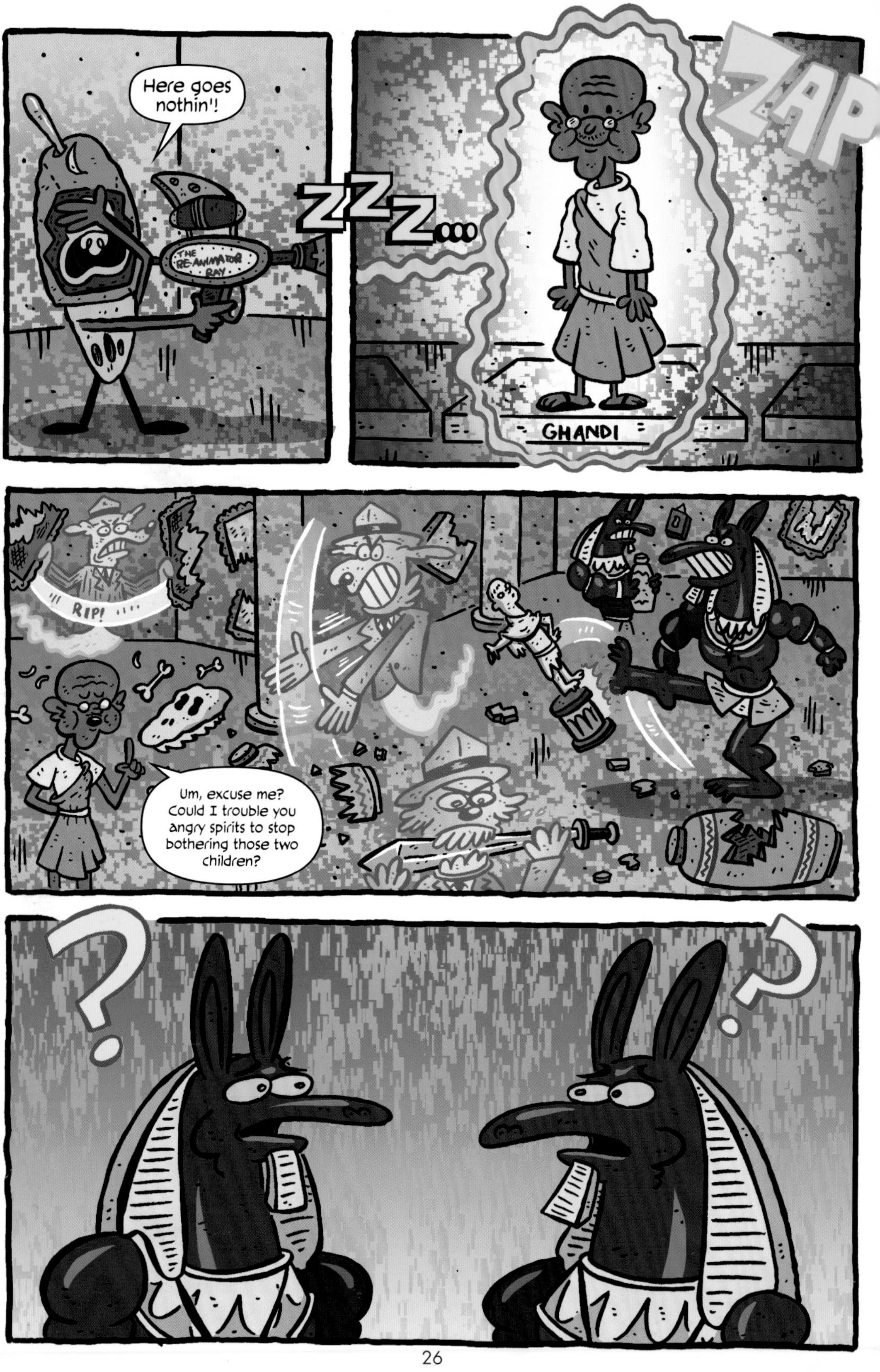
Here goes nothin'!
THE RE-ANIMATOR RAY
ZZZ...
ZAP
GHANDI
RIP!
Um, excuse me? Could I trouble you angry spirits to stop bothering those two children?
?
?

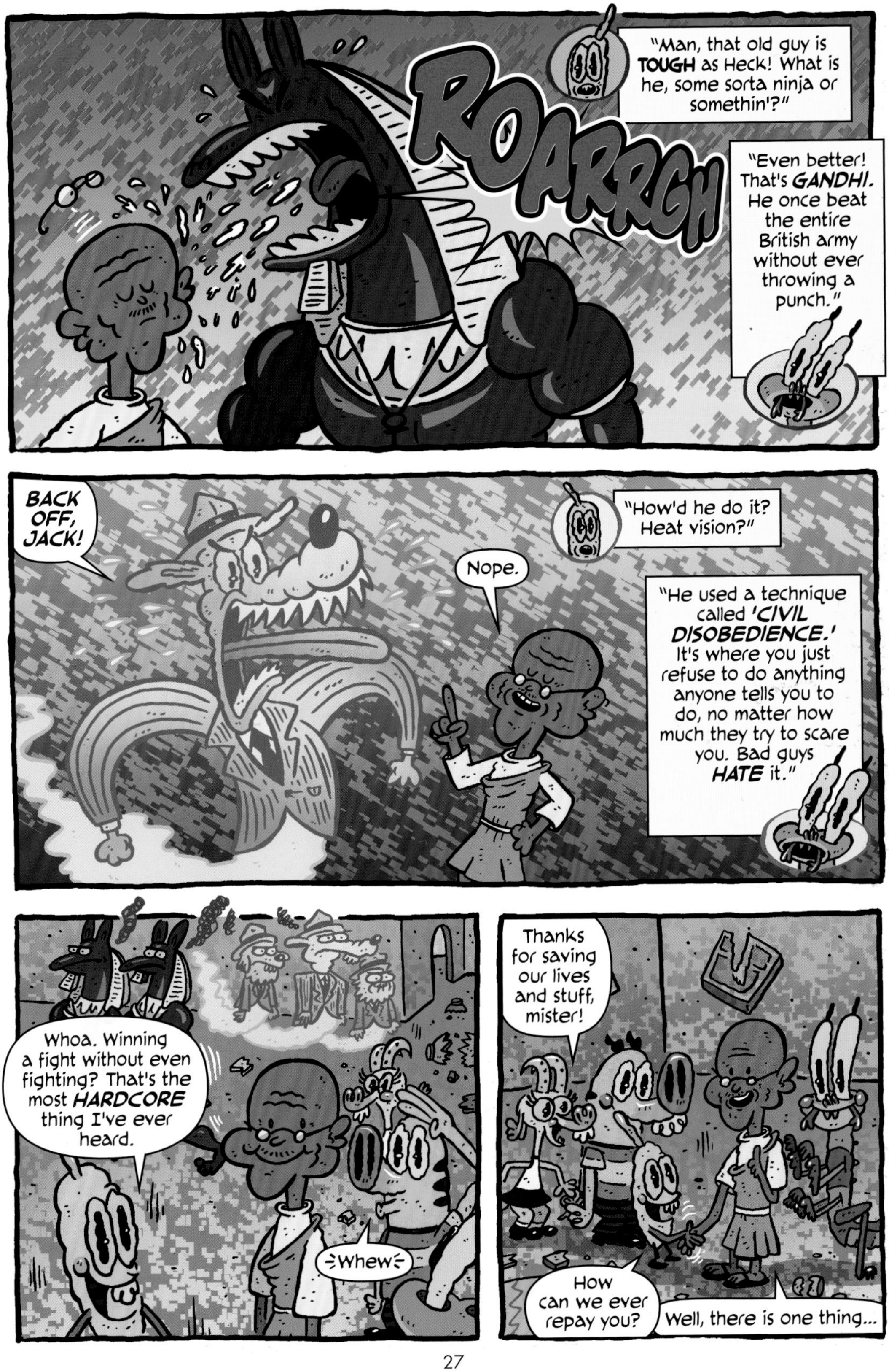
"Man, that old guy is TOUGH as Heck! What is he, some sorta ninja or somethin'?"
ROARRGH
"Even better! That's GANDHI. He once beat the entire British army without ever throwing a punch."
BACK OFF, JACK!
"How'd he do it? Heat vision?"
Nope.
"He used a technique called 'CIVIL DISOBEDIENCE.' It's where you just refuse to do anything anyone tells you to do, no matter how much they try to scare you. Bad guys HATE it."
Whoa. Winning a fight without even fighting? That's the most HARDCORE thing I've ever heard.
Whew
Thanks for saving our lives and stuff, mister!
How can we ever repay you?
Well, there is one thing...

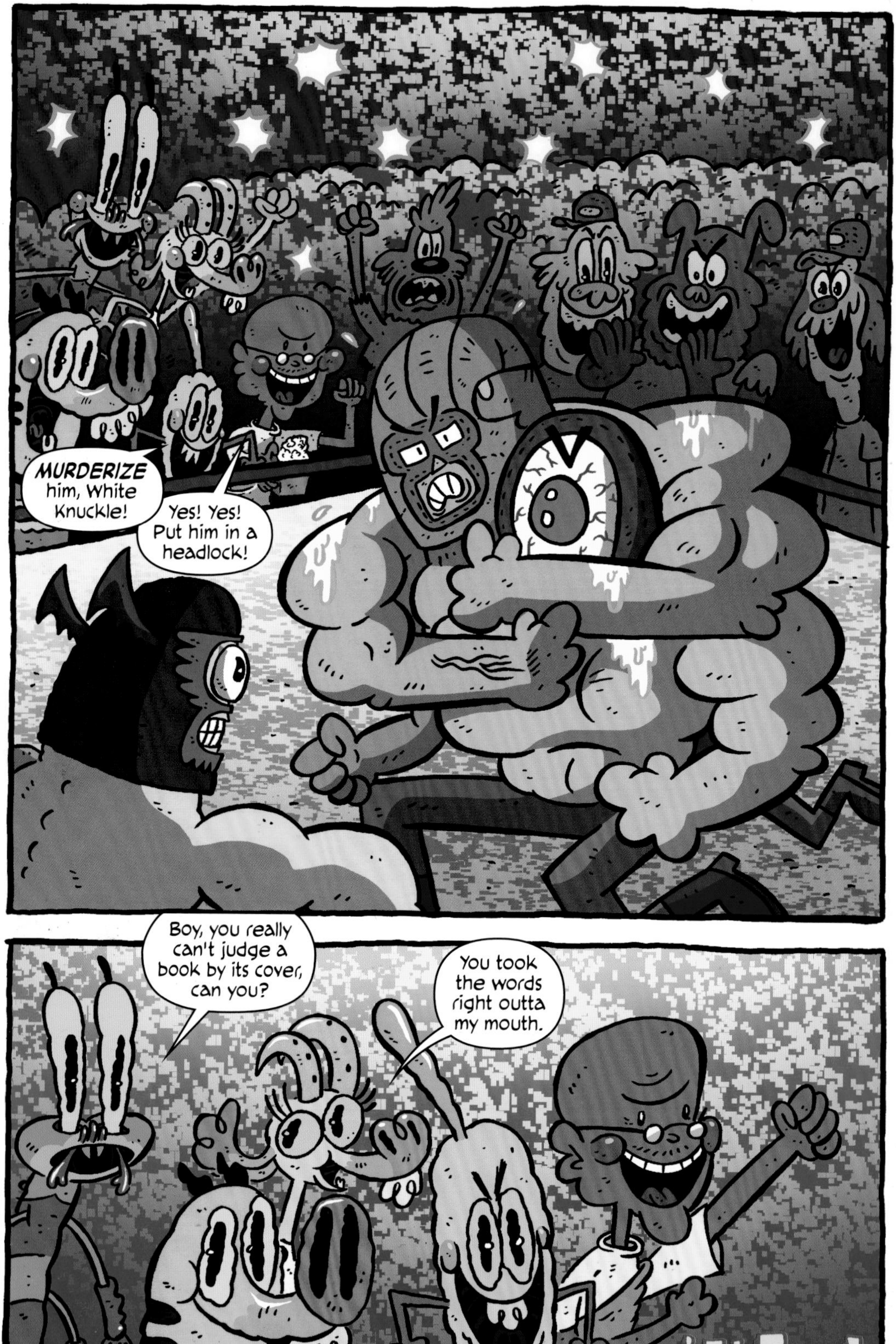
MURDERIZE him, White Knuckle!
Yes! Yes! Put him in a headlock!
Boy, you really can't judge a book by its cover, can you?
You took the words right outta my mouth.
¡El Fin!

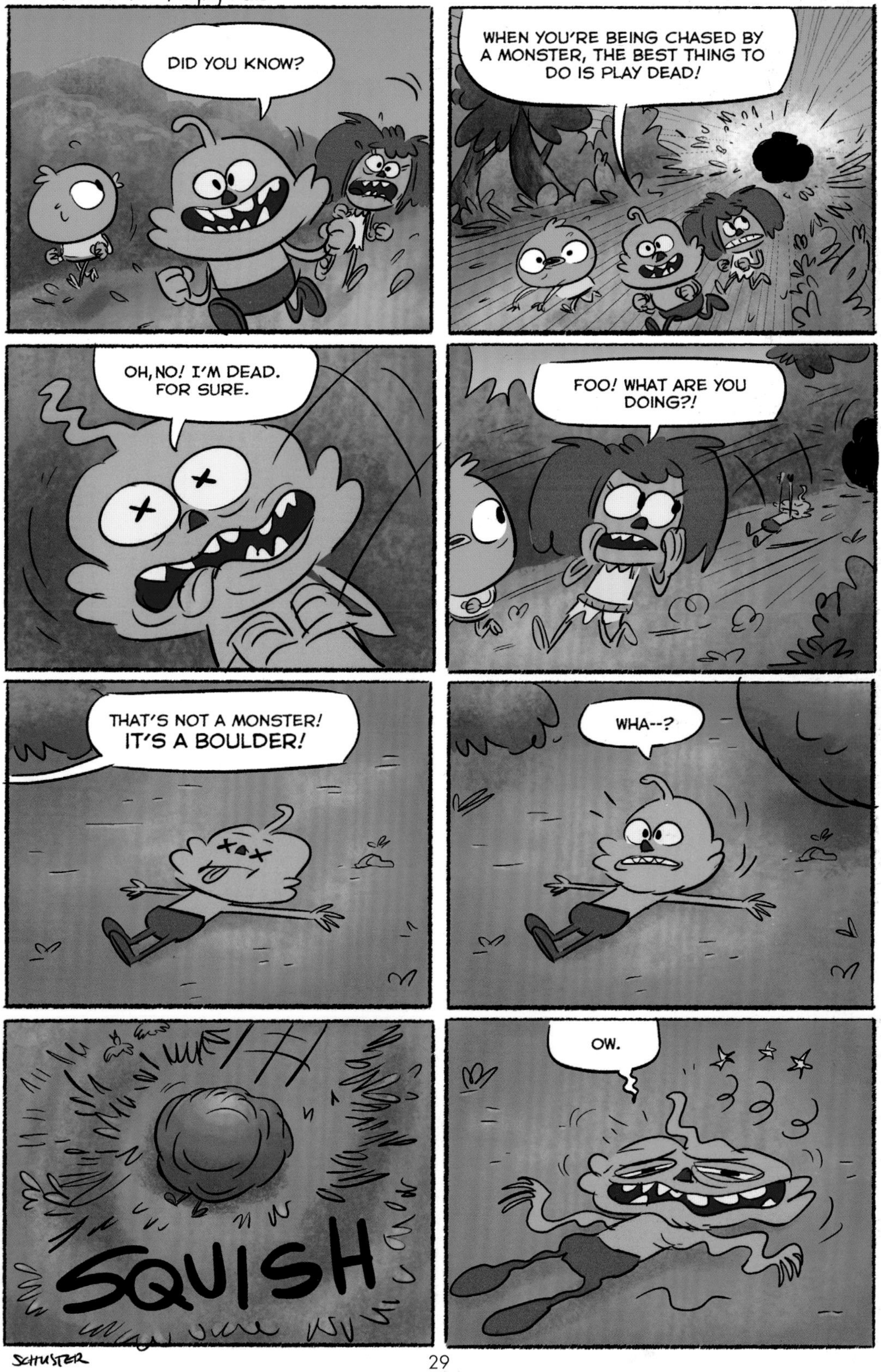
DID YOU KNOW?
WHEN YOU'RE BEING CHASED BY A MONSTER, THE BEST THING TO DO IS PLAY DEAD!
OH, NO! I'M DEAD. FOR SURE.
FOO! WHAT ARE YOU DOING?!
THAT'S NOT A MONSTER! IT'S A BOULDER!
WHA--?
SQUISH
OW.

SCHUSTER

Hee hee! Hahah!

Squirt

Squirt

Dude, wait! LOOK!

VVVVVVVVVmm

WAS THAT WHO I THINK IT WAS?!

It depends...

SANJAY and CRAIG in: the Pensioners

...did you think it was legendary 70's action movie icon CHARLES BUFF HIPS?

YES! He was TUFFLIPS BE-FORE TUFFLIPS WAS TUFFLIPS!

≋GASP!≋ Tell me you're seeing this!

Vvrrmm

WATER BLASTER

See what? 60's Action Star CHARLTON FROSTEDTIPS drive by your house?!

HE WAS TUFFLIPS BEFORE BUFFLIPS WAS TUFFLIPS!

What's going ON?

I think it's pretty clear.

You do?

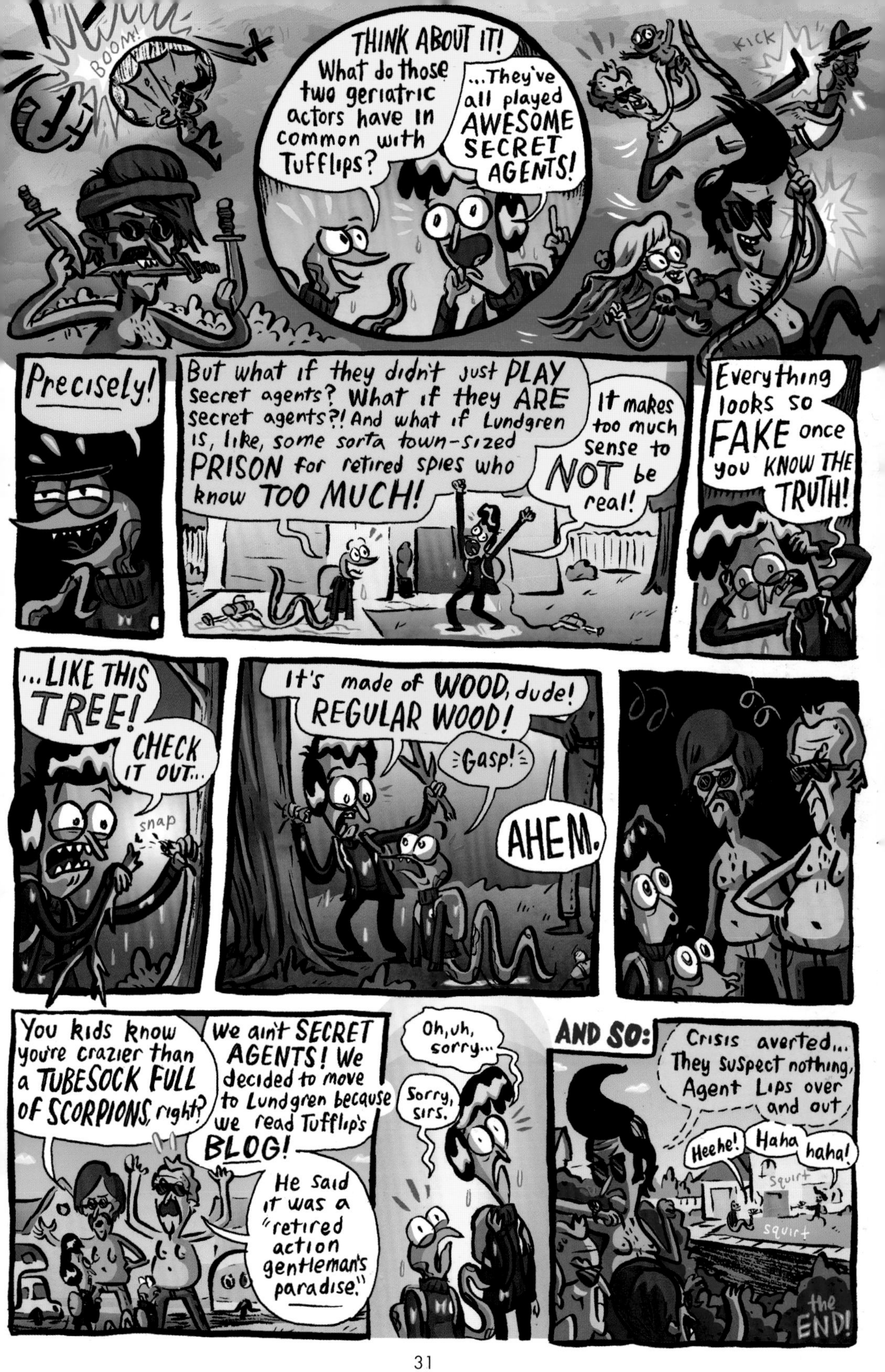
BOOM!
THINK ABOUT IT! What do those two geriatric actors have in common with Tufflips?
...They've all played AWESOME SECRET AGENTS!
KICK
Precisely!
But what if they didn't just PLAY secret agents? What if they ARE secret agents?! And what if Lundgren is, like, some sorta town-sized PRISON for retired spies who know TOO MUCH!
It makes too much sense to NOT be real!
Everything looks so FAKE once you KNOW THE TRUTH!
...LIKE THIS TREE!
CHECK IT OUT...
snap
It's made of WOOD, dude! REGULAR WOOD!
Gasp!
AHEM.
You kids know you're crazier than a TUBESOCK FULL OF SCORPIONS, right?
We ain't SECRET AGENTS! We decided to move to Lundgren because we read Tufflip's BLOG!
He said it was a "retired action gentleman's paradise."
Oh, uh, sorry...
Sorry, sirs.
AND SO:
Crisis averted... They suspect nothing. Agent Lips over and out
Heehe!
Haha
haha!
squirt
squirt
the END!

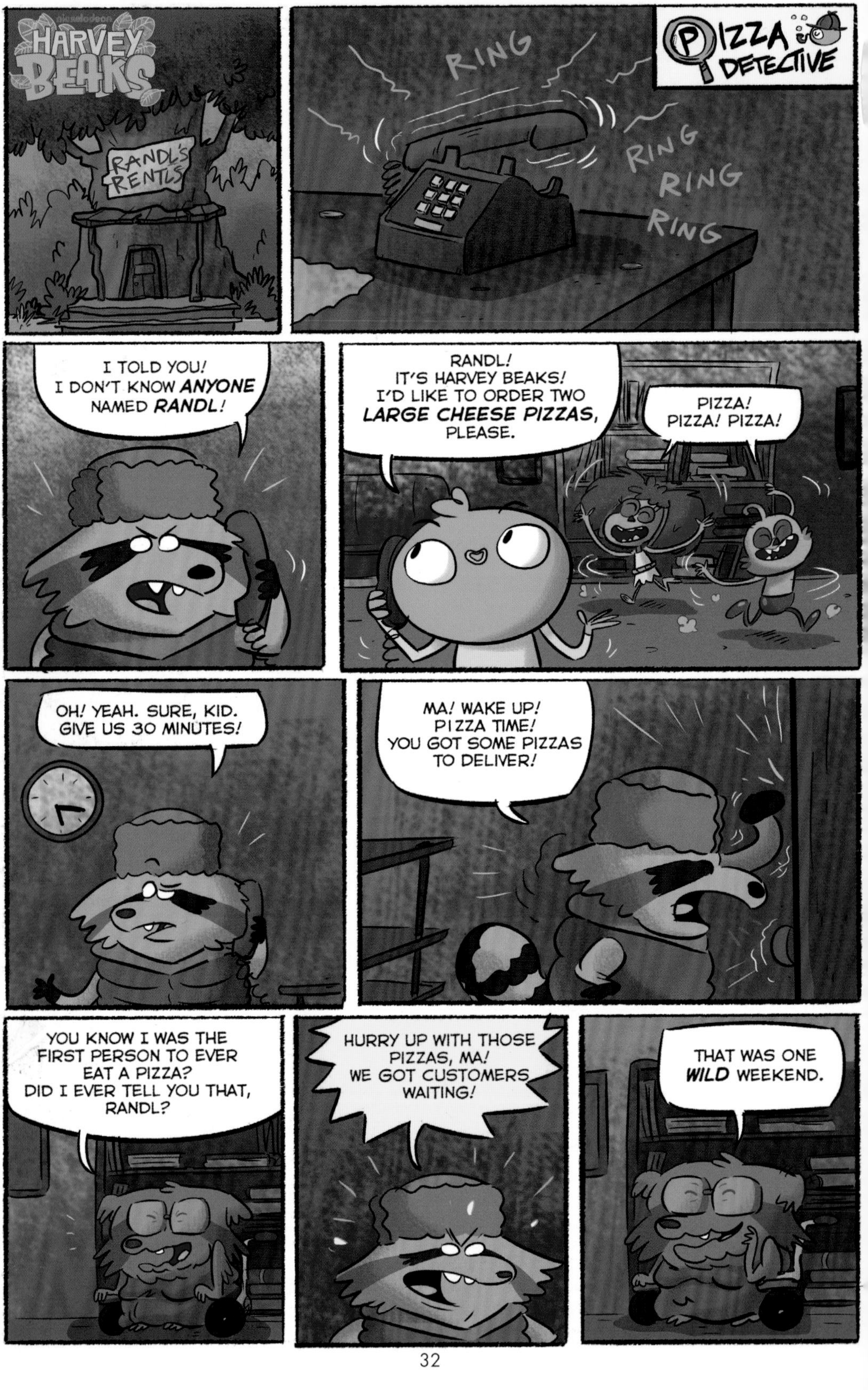
HARVEY BEAKS
RANDL'S RENTLS
PIZZA DETECTIVE
RING
RING
RING
RING
I TOLD YOU! I DON'T KNOW ANYONE NAMED RANDL!
RANDL! IT'S HARVEY BEAKS! I'D LIKE TO ORDER TWO LARGE CHEESE PIZZAS, PLEASE.
PIZZA! PIZZA! PIZZA!
OH! YEAH. SURE, KID. GIVE US 30 MINUTES!
MA! WAKE UP! PIZZA TIME! YOU GOT SOME PIZZAS TO DELIVER!
YOU KNOW I WAS THE FIRST PERSON TO EVER EAT A PIZZA? DID I EVER TELL YOU THAT, RANDL?
HURRY UP WITH THOSE PIZZAS, MA! WE GOT CUSTOMERS WAITING!
THAT WAS ONE WILD WEEKEND.

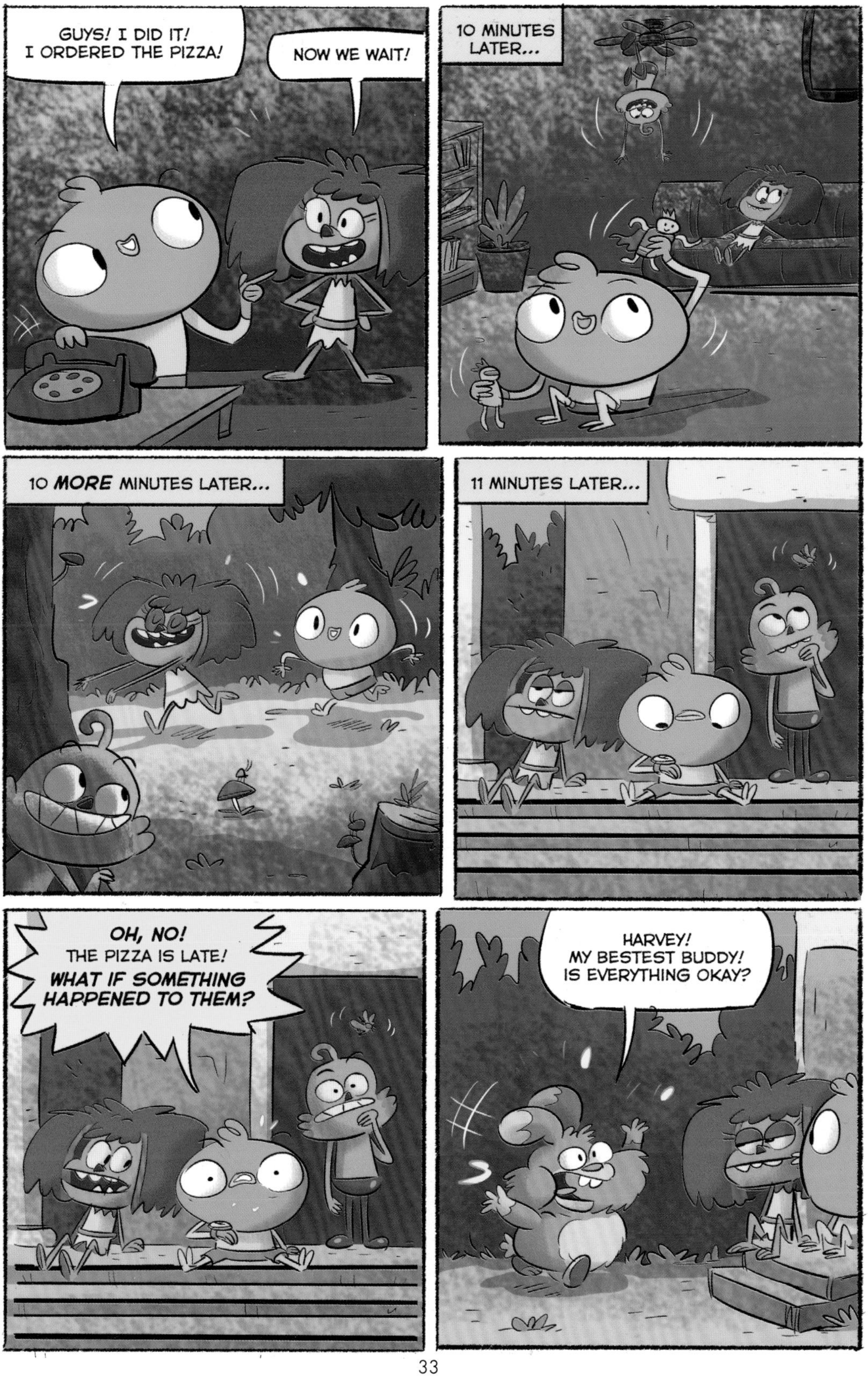
GUYS! I DID IT! I ORDERED THE PIZZA!
NOW WE WAIT!
10 MINUTES LATER...
10 MORE MINUTES LATER...
11 MINUTES LATER...
OH, NO! THE PIZZA IS LATE! WHAT IF SOMETHING HAPPENED TO THEM?
HARVEY! MY BESTEST BUDDY! IS EVERYTHING OKAY?

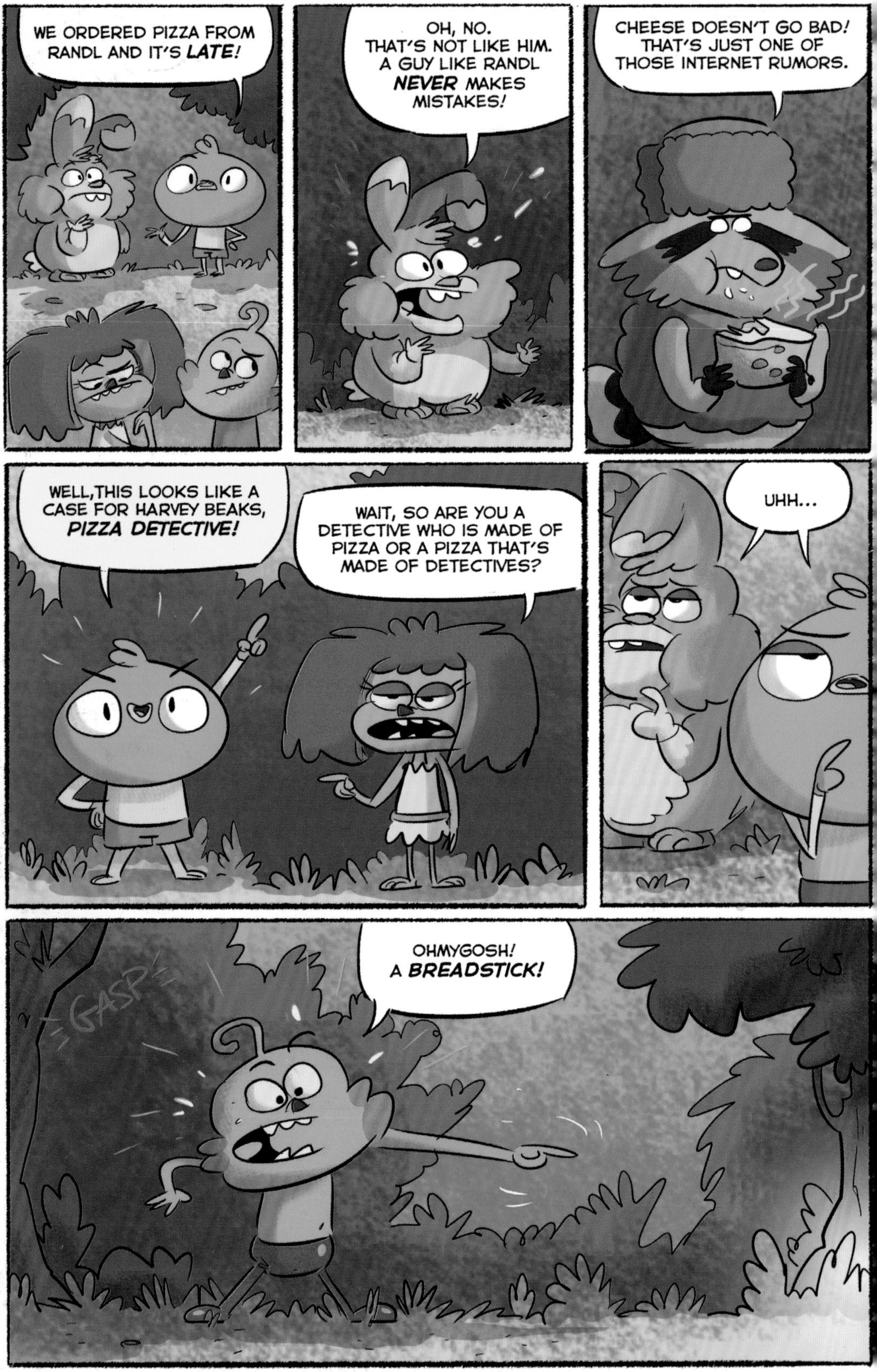
WE ORDERED PIZZA FROM RANDL AND IT'S LATE!
OH, NO. THAT'S NOT LIKE HIM. A GUY LIKE RANDL NEVER MAKES MISTAKES!
CHEESE DOESN'T GO BAD! THAT'S JUST ONE OF THOSE INTERNET RUMORS.
WELL,THIS LOOKS LIKE A CASE FOR HARVEY BEAKS, PIZZA DETECTIVE!
WAIT, SO ARE YOU A DETECTIVE WHO IS MADE OF PIZZA OR A PIZZA THAT'S MADE OF DETECTIVES?
UHH...
GASP
OHMYGOSH! A BREADSTICK!

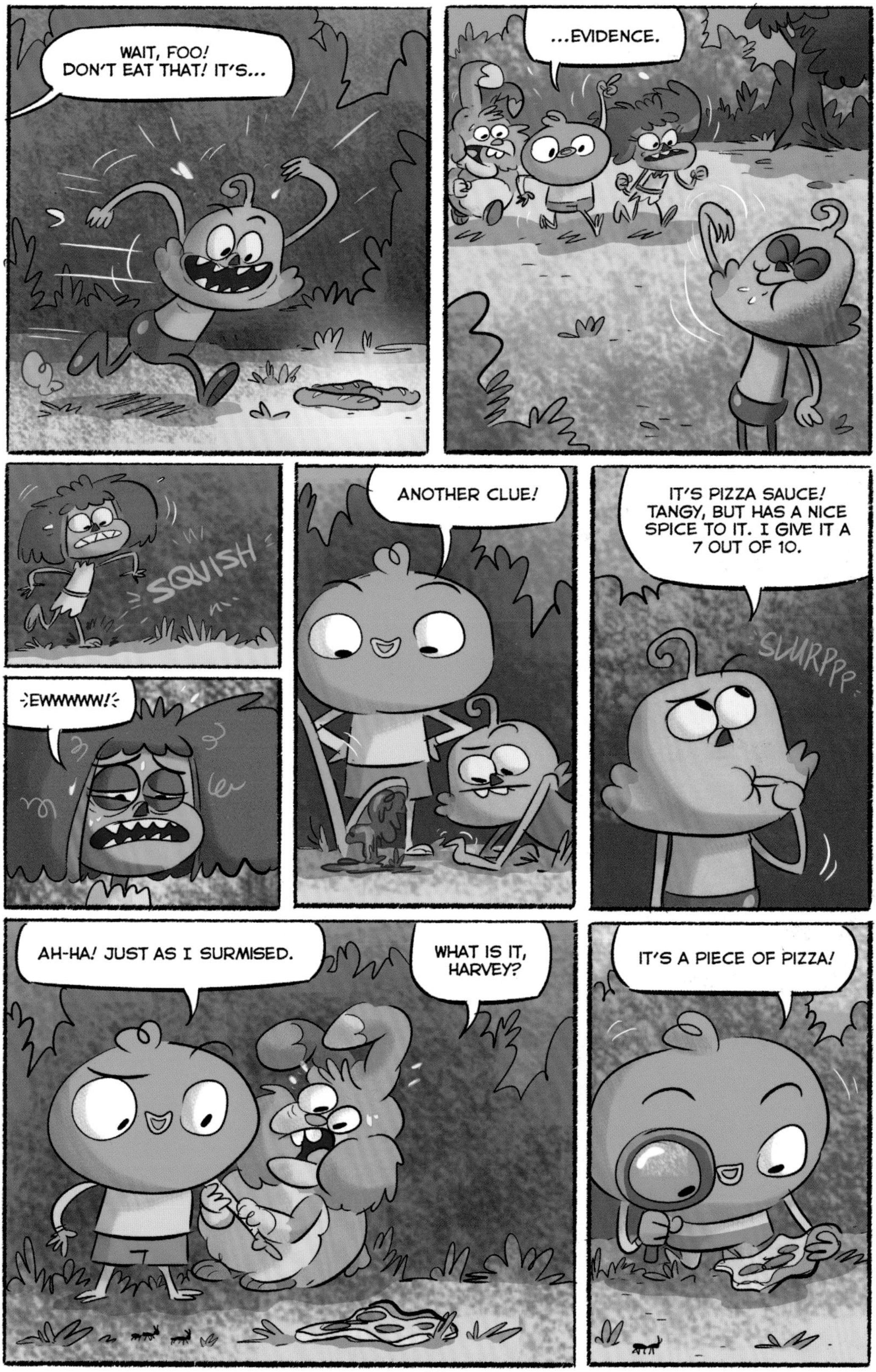

WAIT, FOO! DON'T EAT THAT! IT'S...
...EVIDENCE.
SQUISH
:EWWWWW!:
ANOTHER CLUE!
IT'S PIZZA SAUCE! TANGY, BUT HAS A NICE SPICE TO IT. I GIVE IT A 7 OUT OF 10.
SLURPPP
AH-HA! JUST AS I SURMISED.
WHAT IS IT, HARVEY?
IT'S A PIECE OF PIZZA!

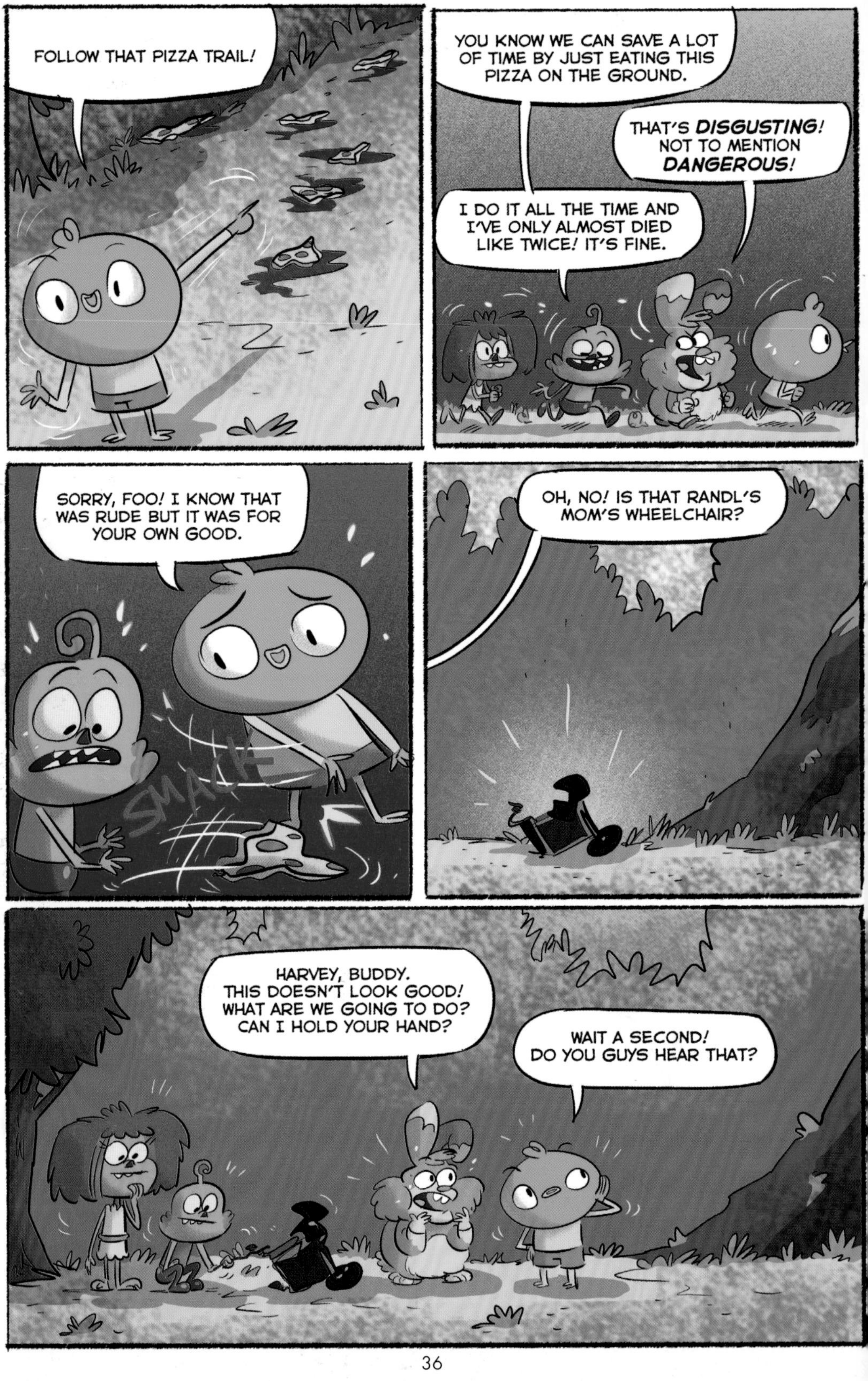
FOLLOW THAT PIZZA TRAIL!
YOU KNOW WE CAN SAVE A LOT OF TIME BY JUST EATING THIS PIZZA ON THE GROUND.
THAT'S DISGUSTING! NOT TO MENTION DANGEROUS!
I DO IT ALL THE TIME AND I'VE ONLY ALMOST DIED LIKE TWICE! IT'S FINE.
SORRY, FOO! I KNOW THAT WAS RUDE BUT IT WAS FOR YOUR OWN GOOD.
SMACK
OH, NO! IS THAT RANDL'S MOM'S WHEELCHAIR?
HARVEY, BUDDY. THIS DOESN'T LOOK GOOD! WHAT ARE WE GOING TO DO? CAN I HOLD YOUR HAND?
WAIT A SECOND! DO YOU GUYS HEAR THAT?

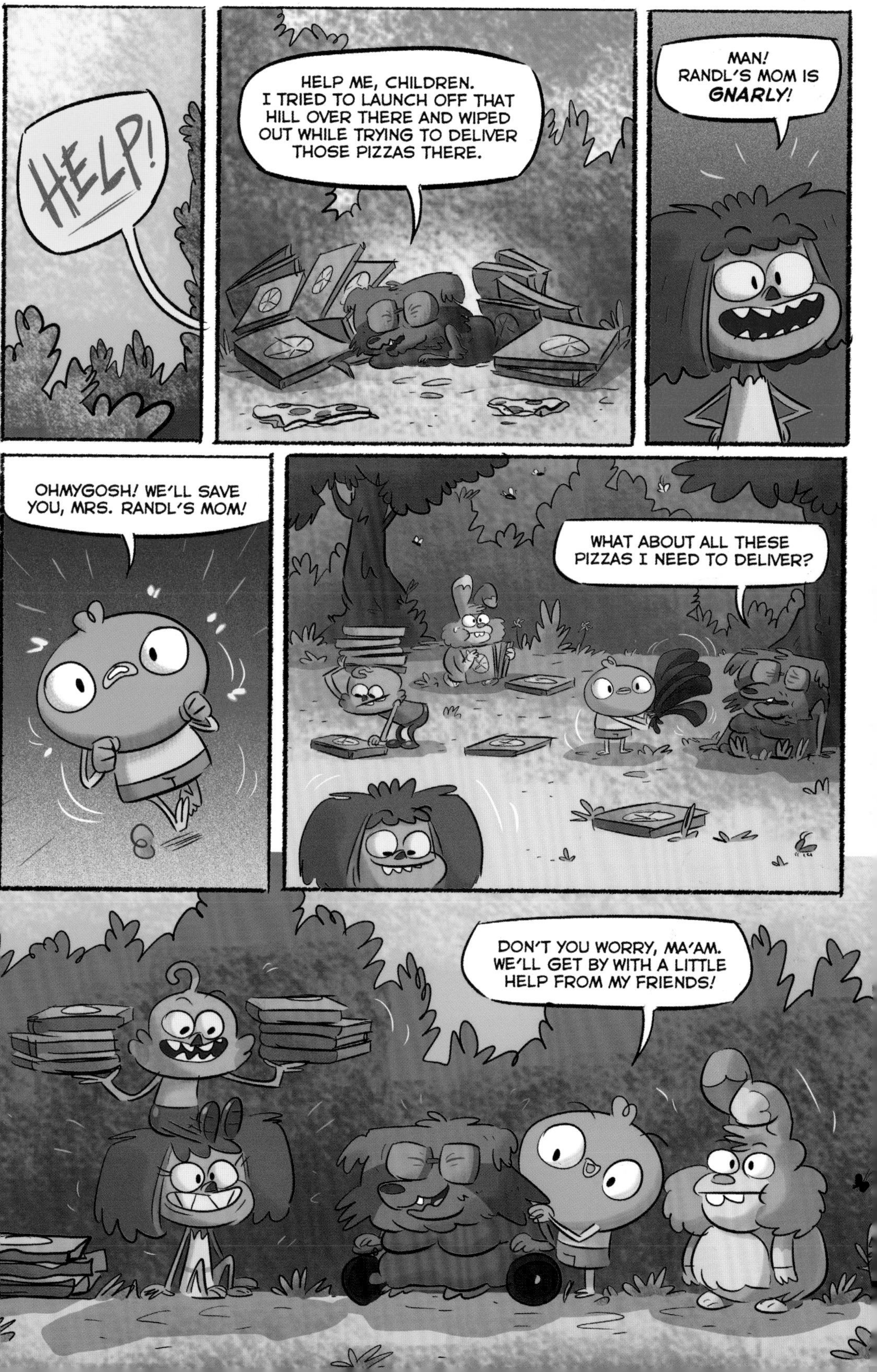
HELP!
HELP ME, CHILDREN. I TRIED TO LAUNCH OFF THAT HILL OVER THERE AND WIPED OUT WHILE TRYING TO DELIVER THOSE PIZZAS THERE.
MAN! RANDL'S MOM IS GNARLY!
OHMYGOSH! WE'LL SAVE YOU, MRS. RANDL'S MOM!
WHAT ABOUT ALL THESE PIZZAS I NEED TO DELIVER?
DON'T YOU WORRY, MA'AM. WE'LL GET BY WITH A LITTLE HELP FROM MY FRIENDS!

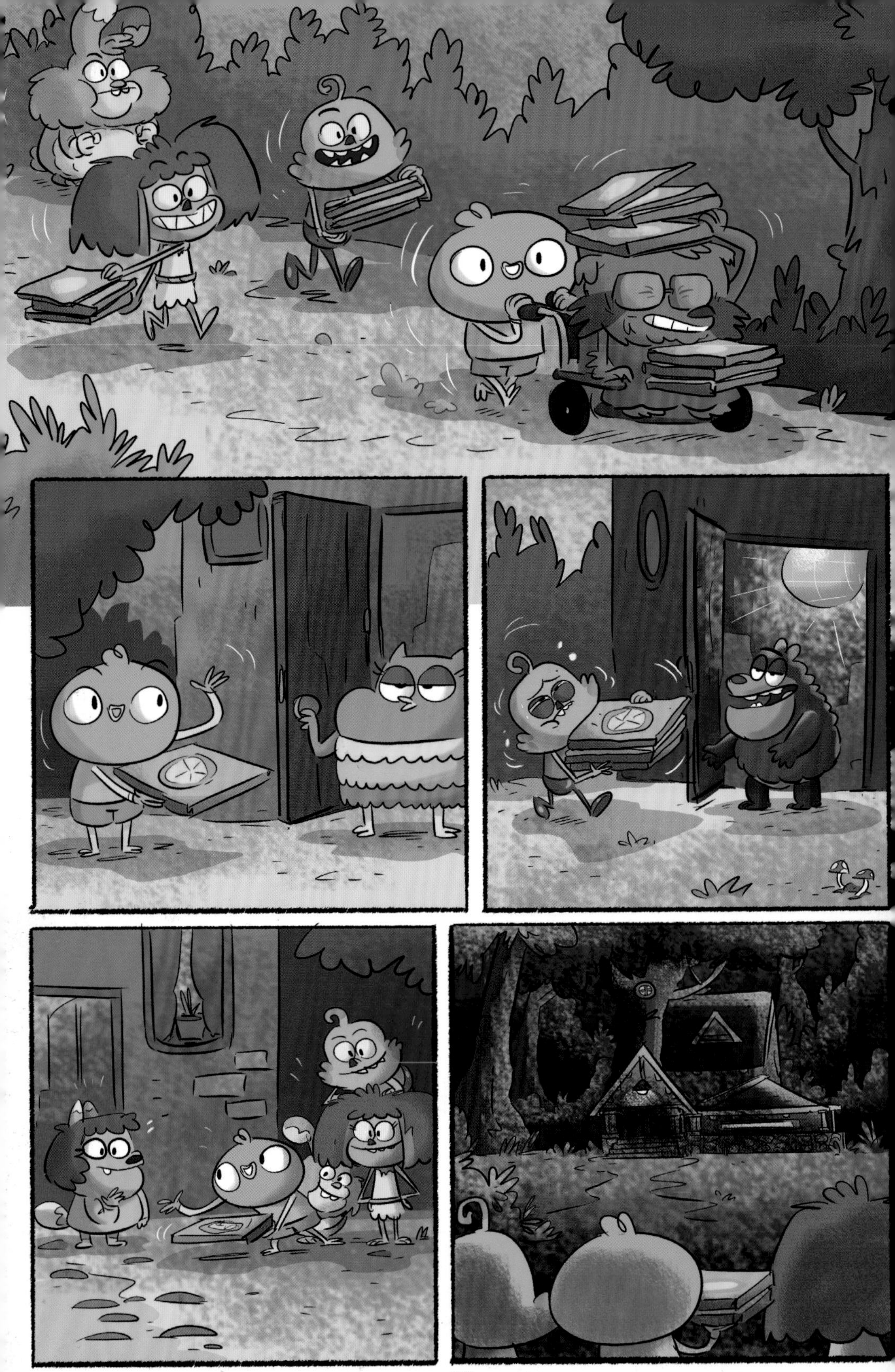

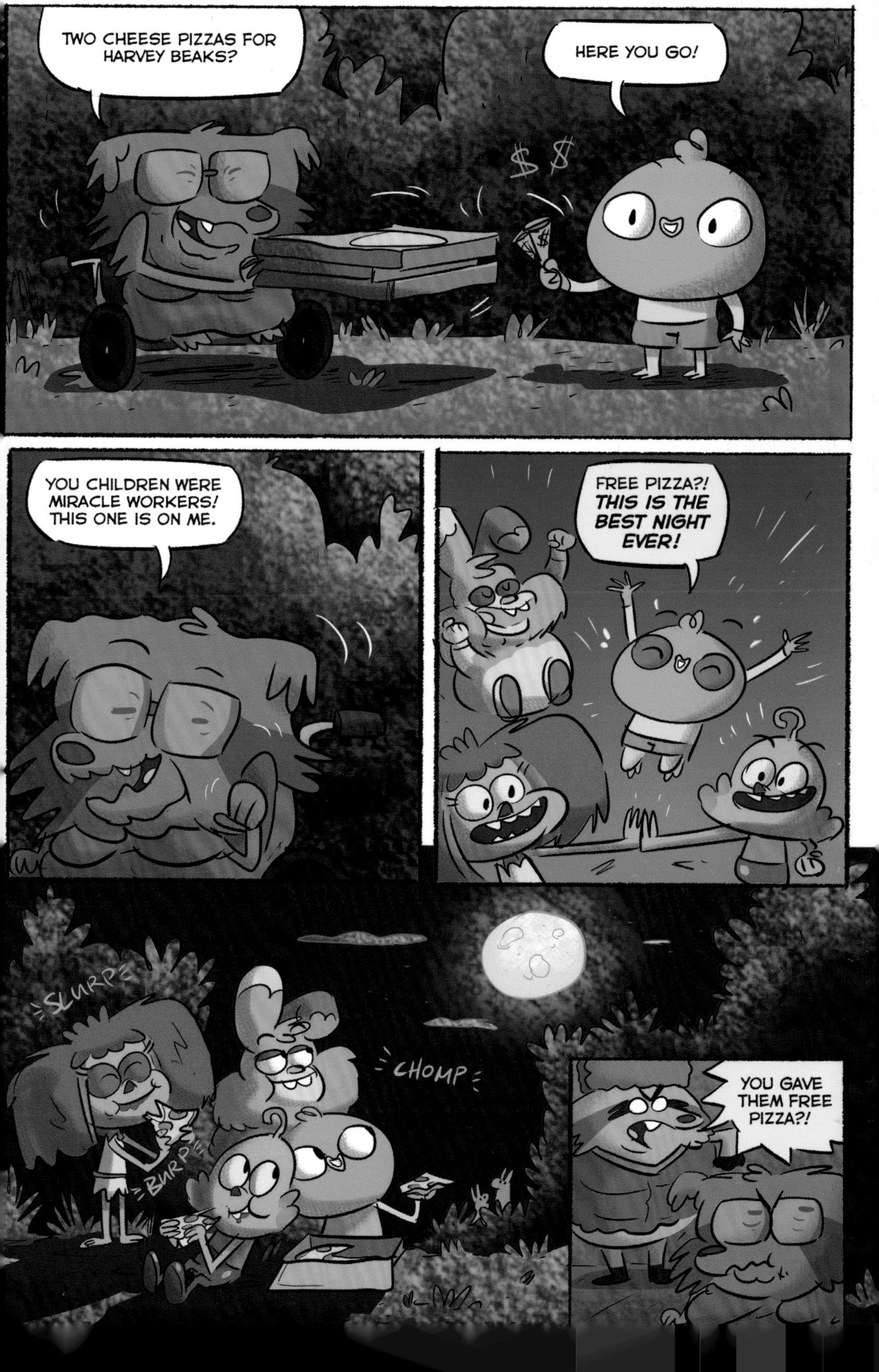

TWO CHEESE PIZZAS FOR HARVEY BEAKS?
HERE YOU GO!
$ $
YOU CHILDREN WERE MIRACLE WORKERS! THIS ONE IS ON ME.
FREE PIZZA?! THIS IS THE BEST NIGHT EVER!
SLURPE
CHOMP
BURP
YOU GAVE THEM FREE PIZZA?!

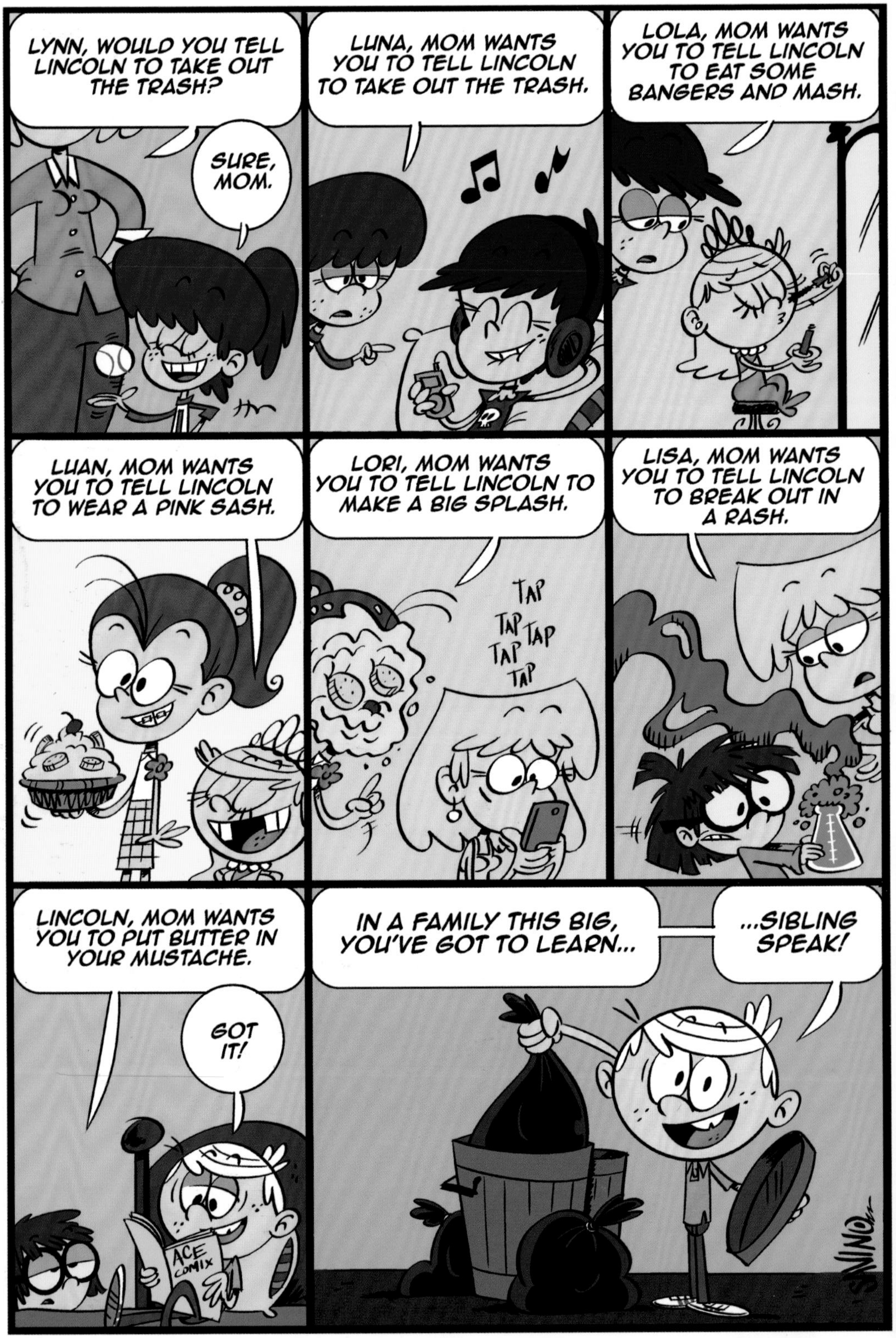
LYNN, WOULD YOU TELL LINCOLN TO TAKE OUT THE TRASH?
SURE, MOM.
LUNA, MOM WANTS YOU TO TELL LINCOLN TO TAKE OUT THE TRASH.
LOLA, MOM WANTS YOU TO TELL LINCOLN TO EAT SOME BANGERS AND MASH.
LUAN, MOM WANTS YOU TO TELL LINCOLN TO WEAR A PINK SASH.
LORI, MOM WANTS YOU TO TELL LINCOLN TO MAKE A BIG SPLASH.
TAP TAP TAP TAP TAP
LISA, MOM WANTS YOU TO TELL LINCOLN TO BREAK OUT IN A RASH.
LINCOLN, MOM WANTS YOU TO PUT BUTTER IN YOUR MUSTACHE.
GOT IT!
ACE COMIX
IN A FAMILY THIS BIG, YOU'VE GOT TO LEARN...
...SIBLING SPEAK!

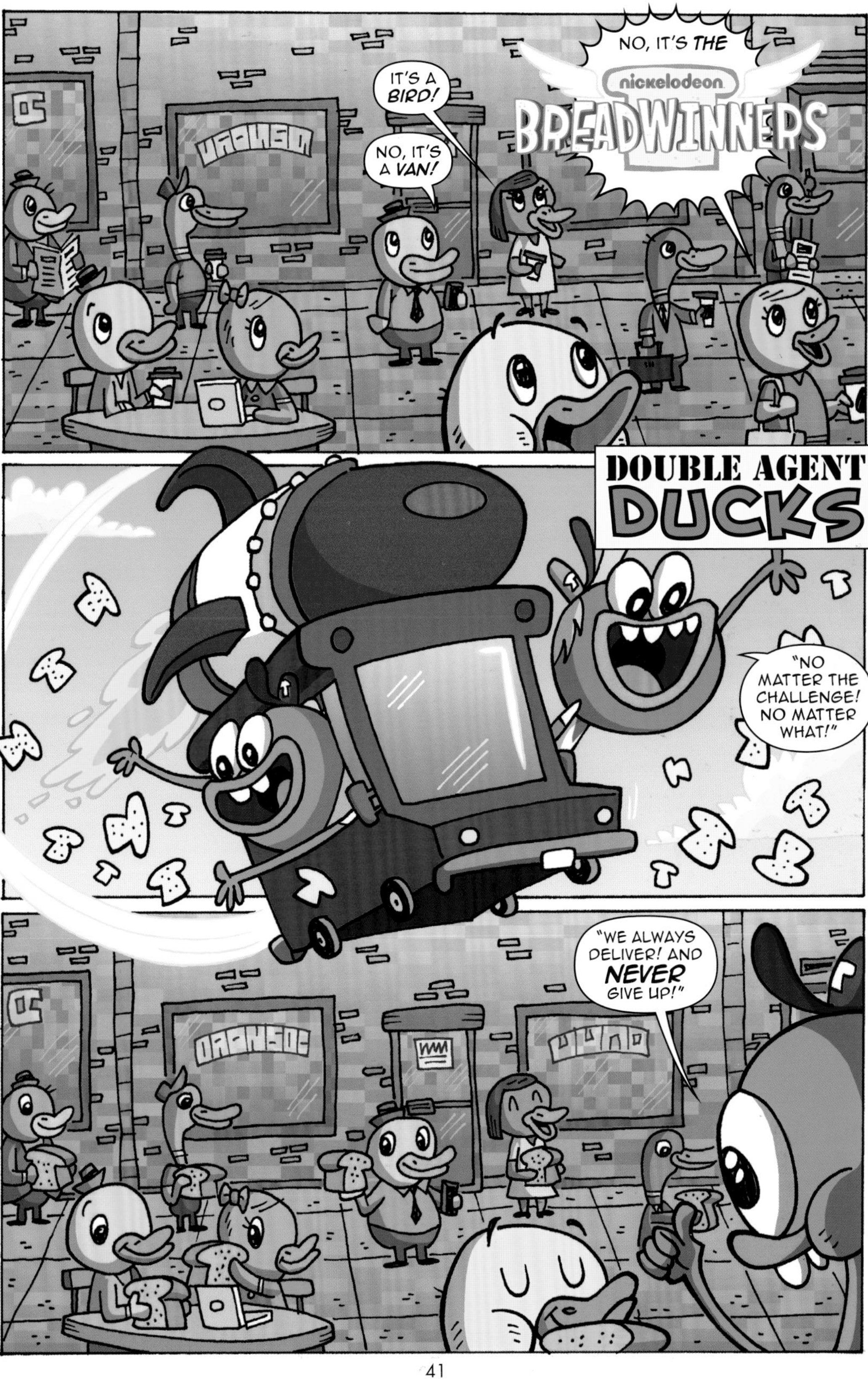
IT'S A BIRD!
NO, IT'S A VAN!
NO, IT'S THE nickelodeon BREADWINNERS
DOUBLE AGENT DUCKS
"NO MATTER THE CHALLENGE! NO MATTER WHAT!"
"WE ALWAYS DELIVER! AND NEVER GIVE UP!"

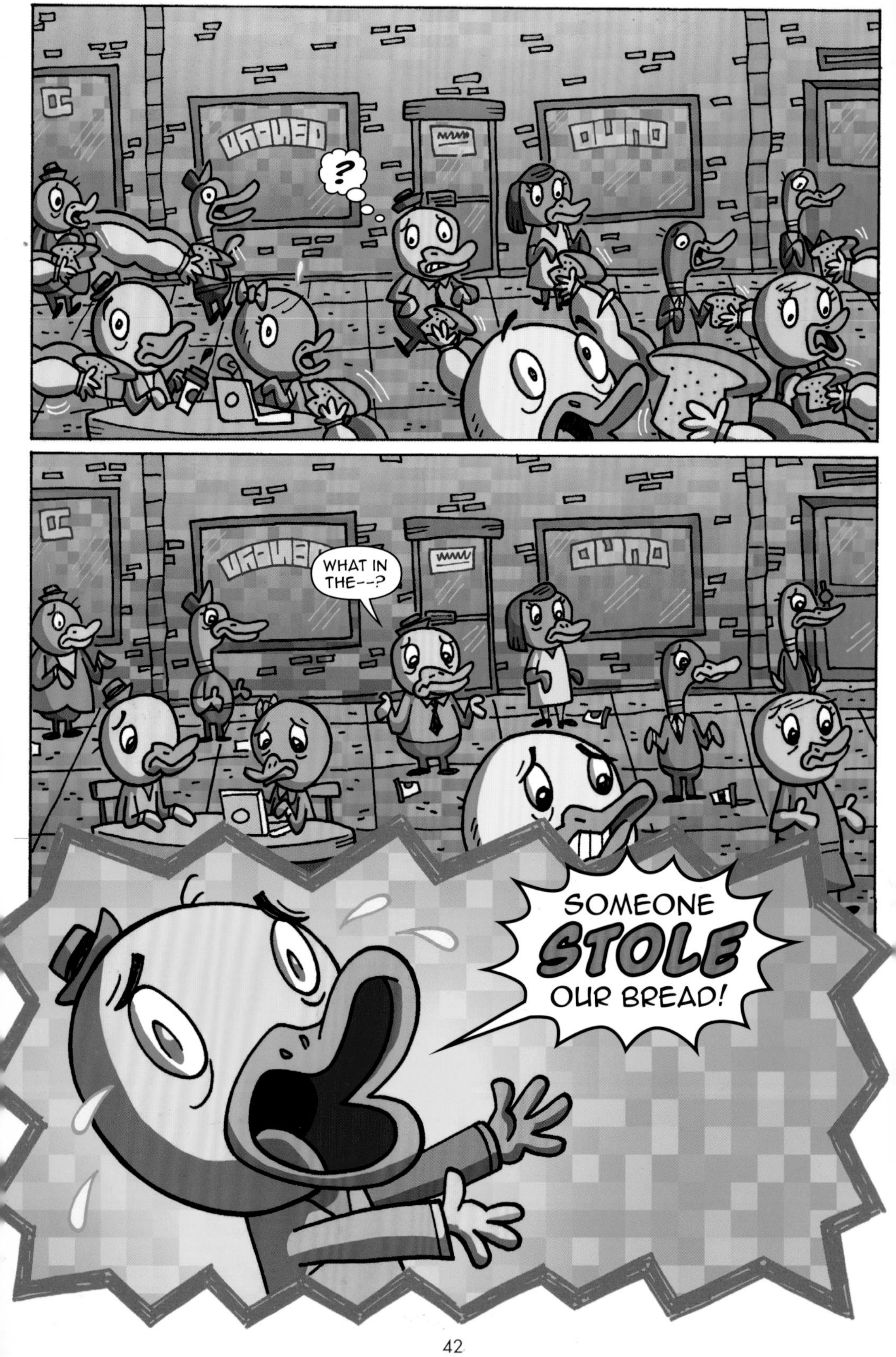
?
WHAT IN THE--?
SOMEONE STOLE OUR BREAD!

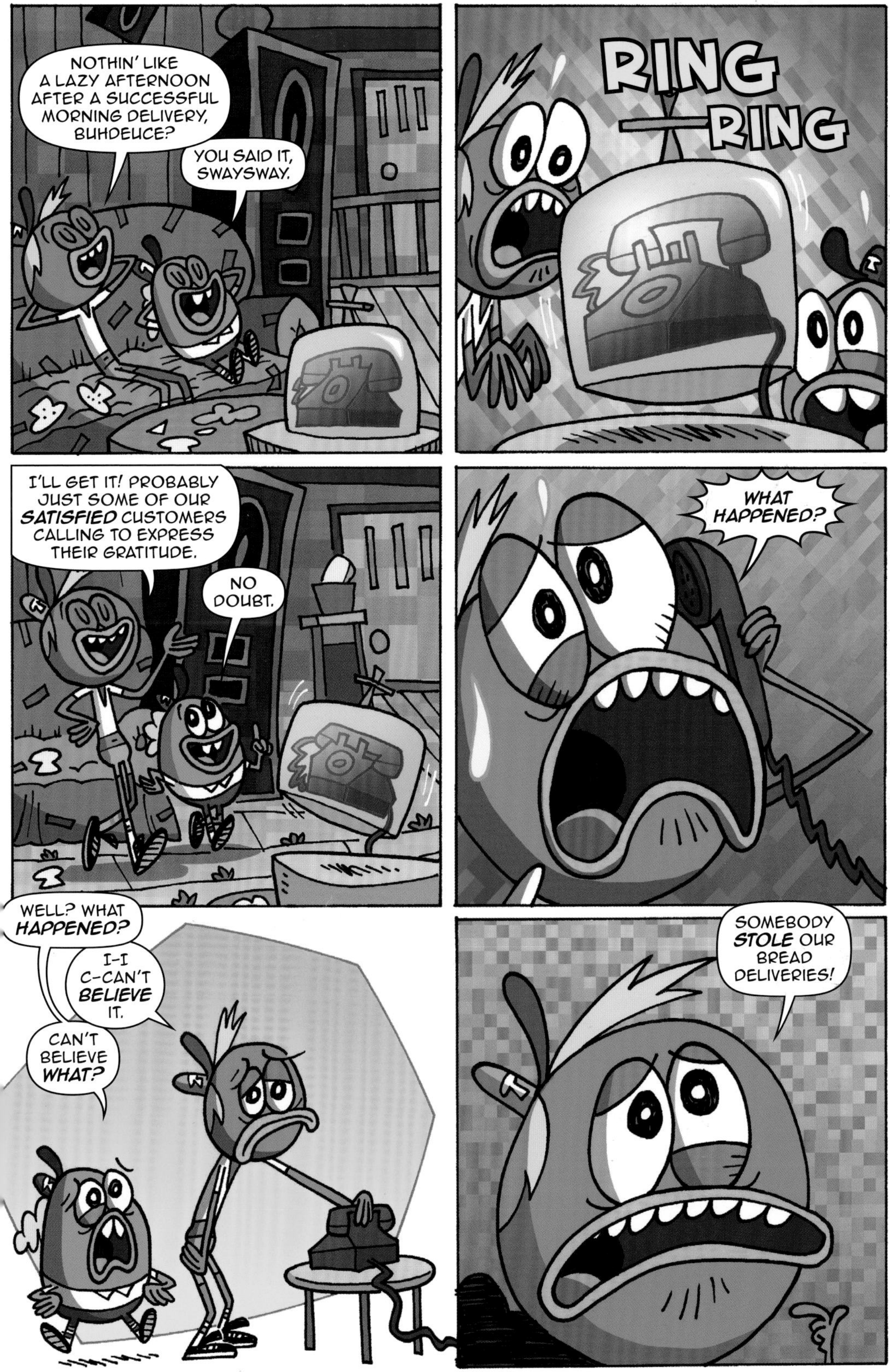
NOTHIN' LIKE A LAZY AFTERNOON AFTER A SUCCESSFUL MORNING DELIVERY, BUHDEUCE?
YOU SAID IT, SWAYSWAY.
RING RING
I'LL GET IT! PROBABLY JUST SOME OF OUR SATISFIED CUSTOMERS CALLING TO EXPRESS THEIR GRATITUDE.
NO DOUBT.
WHAT HAPPENED?
WELL? WHAT HAPPENED?
I-I C-CAN'T BELIEVE IT.
CAN'T BELIEVE WHAT?
SOMEBODY STOLE OUR BREAD DELIVERIES!

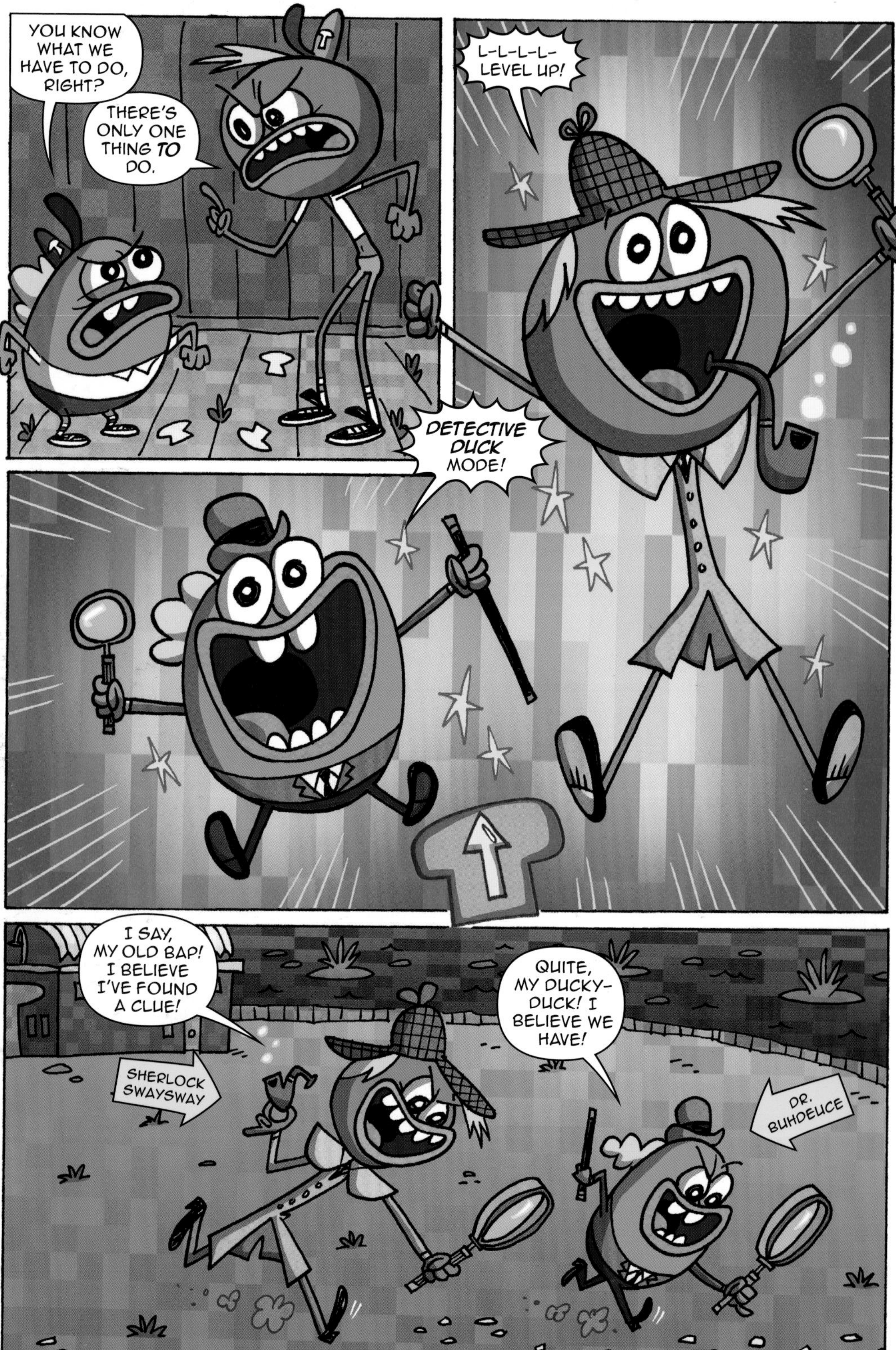
YOU KNOW WHAT WE HAVE TO DO, RIGHT?
THERE'S ONLY ONE THING TO DO.
L-L-L-L-LEVEL UP!
DETECTIVE DUCK MODE!
I SAY, MY OLD BAP! I BELIEVE I'VE FOUND A CLUE!
QUITE, MY DUCKY-DUCK! I BELIEVE WE HAVE!
SHERLOCK SWAYSWAY
DR. BUHDEUCE

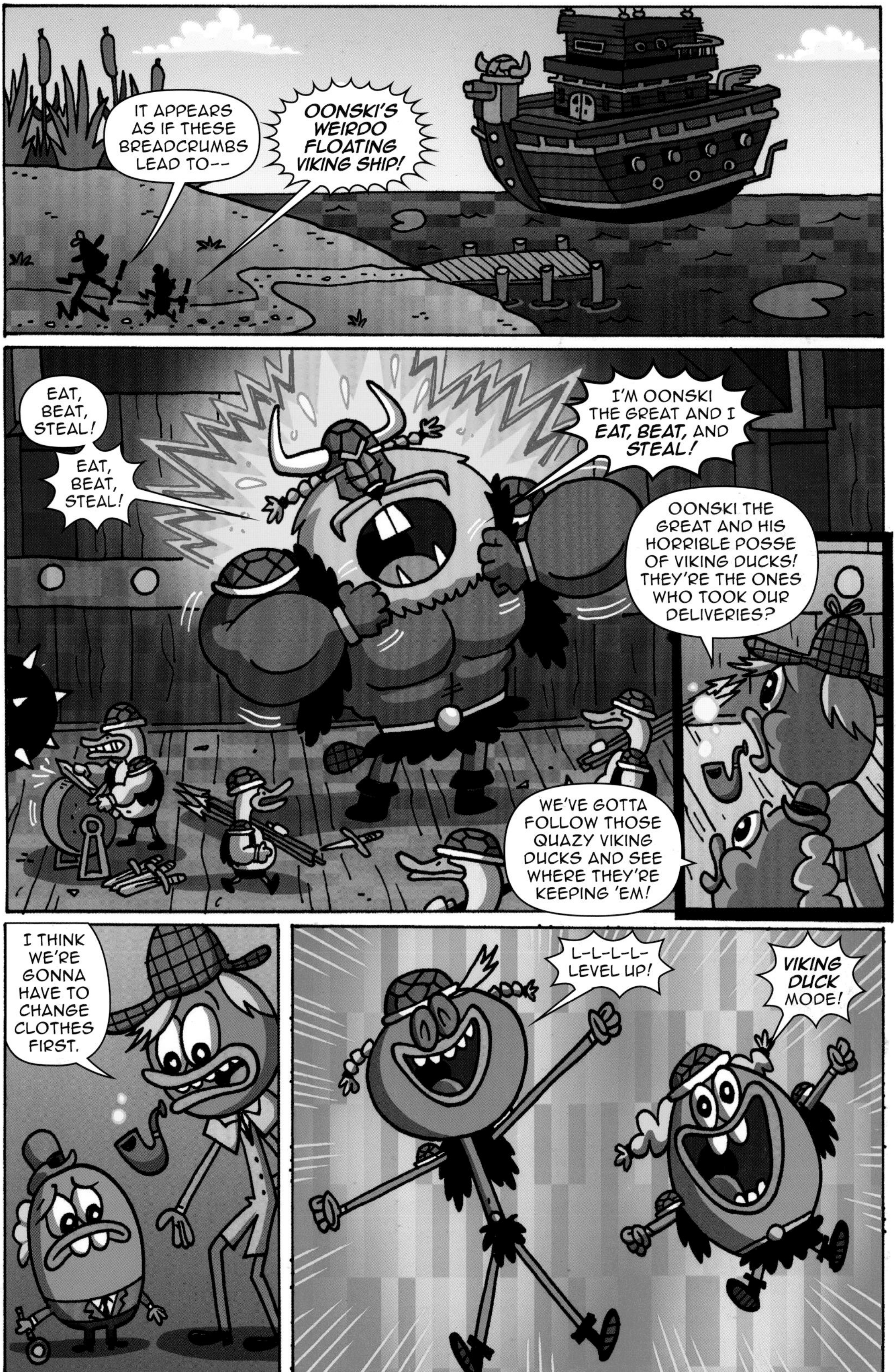
IT APPEARS AS IF THESE BREADCRUMBS LEAD TO--
OONSKI'S WEIRDO FLOATING VIKING SHIP!
EAT, BEAT, STEAL!
EAT, BEAT, STEAL!
I'M OONSKI THE GREAT AND I EAT, BEAT, AND STEAL!
OONSKI THE GREAT AND HIS HORRIBLE POSSE OF VIKING DUCKS! THEY'RE THE ONES WHO TOOK OUR DELIVERIES?
WE'VE GOTTA FOLLOW THOSE QUAZY VIKING DUCKS AND SEE WHERE THEY'RE KEEPING 'EM!
I THINK WE'RE GONNA HAVE TO CHANGE CLOTHES FIRST.
L-L-L-L-LEVEL UP!
VIKING DUCK MODE!

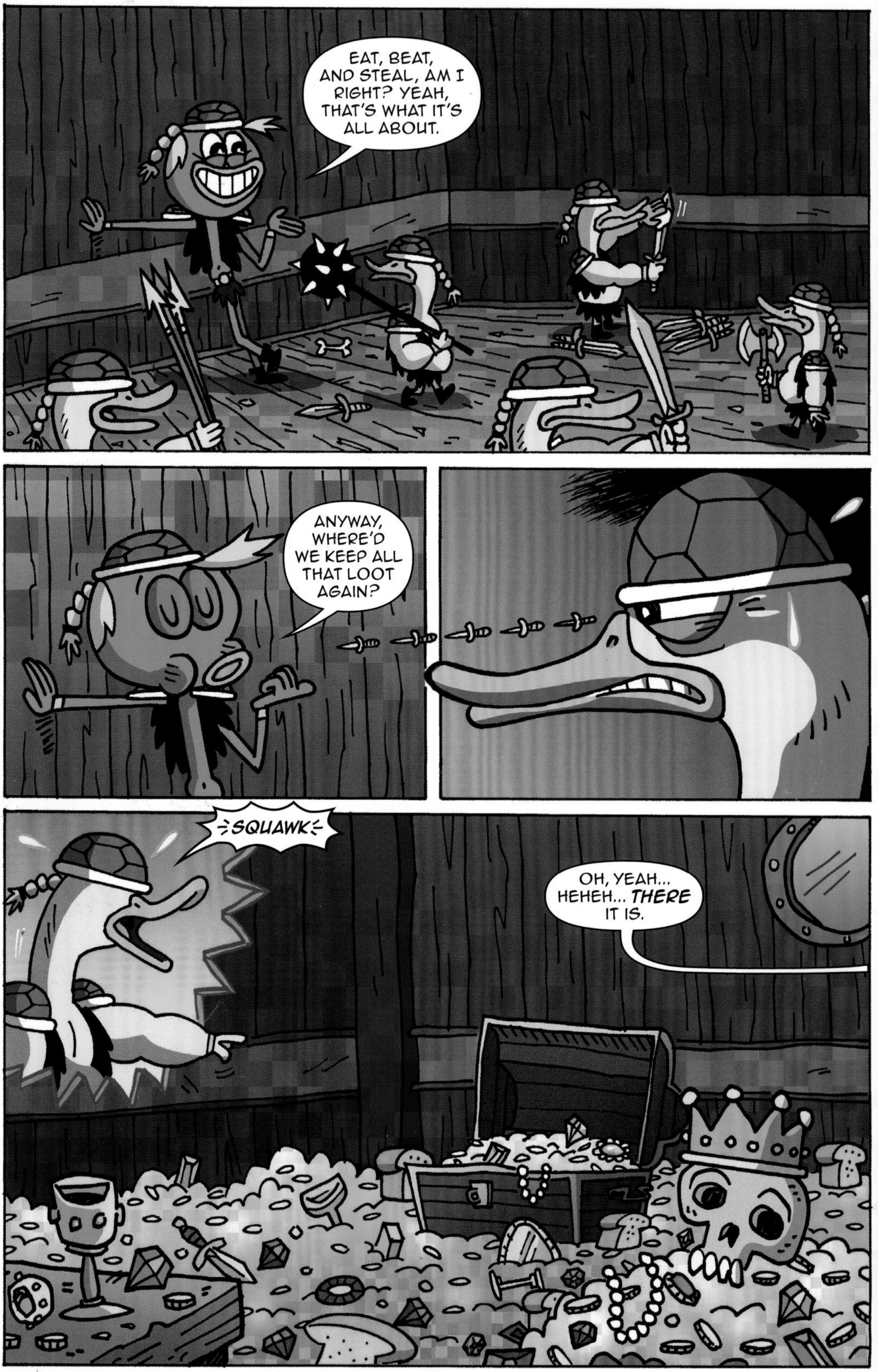
EAT, BEAT, AND STEAL, AM I RIGHT? YEAH, THAT'S WHAT IT'S ALL ABOUT.
ANYWAY, WHERE'D WE KEEP ALL THAT LOOT AGAIN?
SQUAWK
OH, YEAH... HEHEH... *THERE* IT IS.

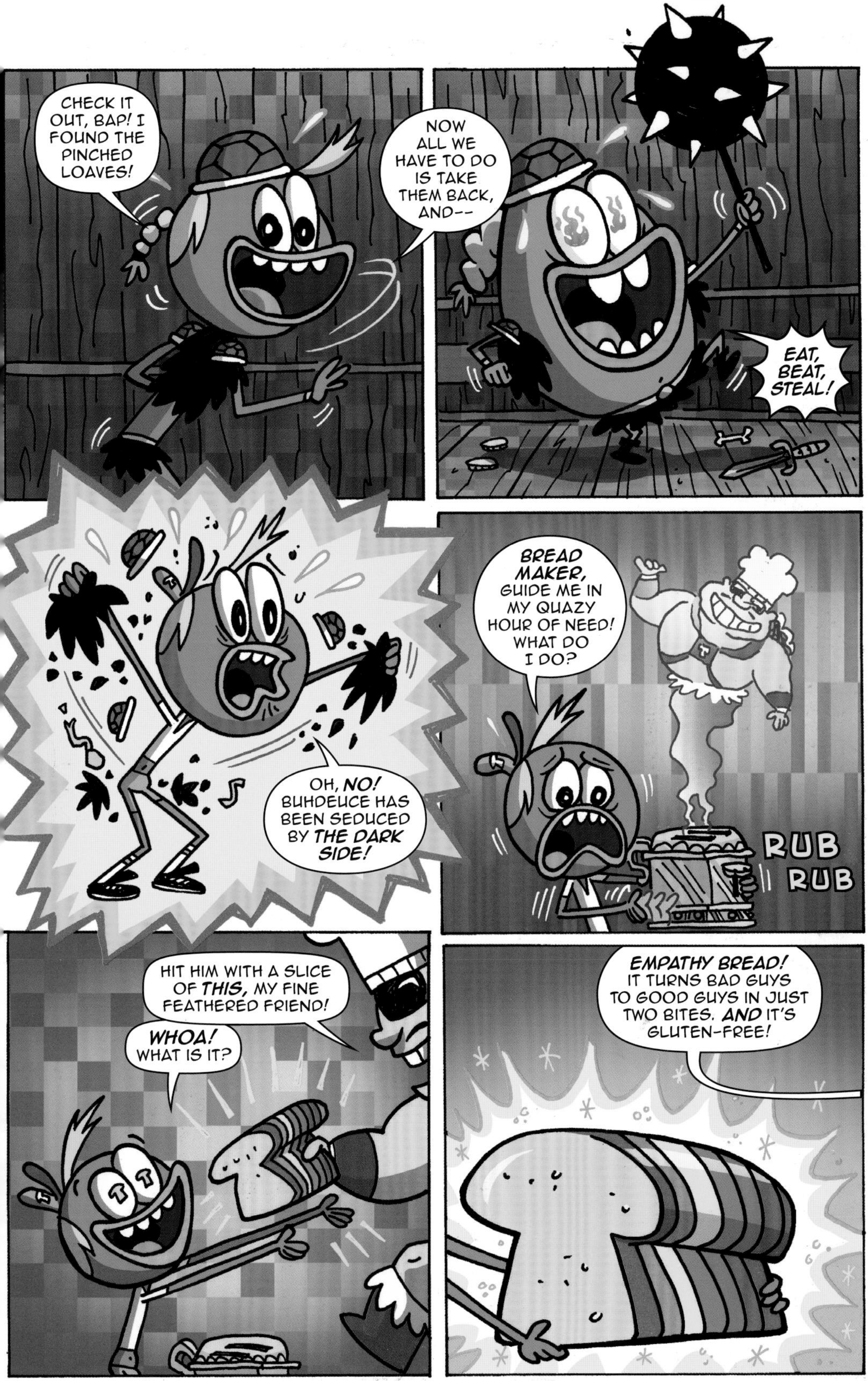
CHECK IT OUT, BAP! I FOUND THE PINCHED LOAVES!
NOW ALL WE HAVE TO DO IS TAKE THEM BACK, AND--
EAT, BEAT, STEAL!
OH, NO! BUHDEUCE HAS BEEN SEDUCED BY THE DARK SIDE!
BREAD MAKER, GUIDE ME IN MY QUAZY HOUR OF NEED! WHAT DO I DO?
RUB RUB
HIT HIM WITH A SLICE OF THIS, MY FINE FEATHERED FRIEND!
WHOA! WHAT IS IT?
EMPATHY BREAD! IT TURNS BAD GUYS TO GOOD GUYS IN JUST TWO BITES. AND IT'S GLUTEN-FREE!

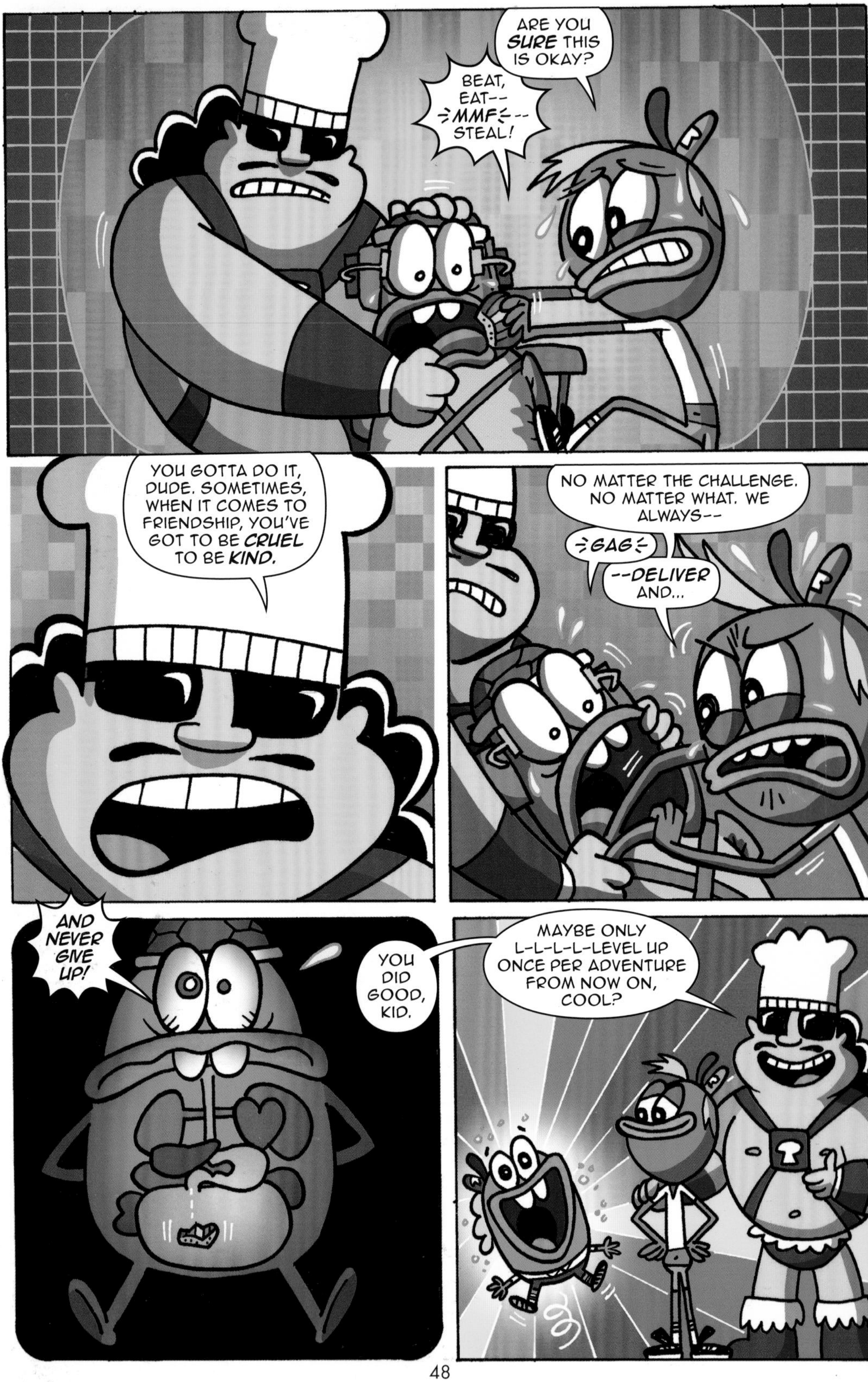
ARE YOU SURE THIS IS OKAY?
BEAT, EAT-- MMF-- STEAL!
YOU GOTTA DO IT, DUDE. SOMETIMES, WHEN IT COMES TO FRIENDSHIP, YOU'VE GOT TO BE CRUEL TO BE KIND.
NO MATTER THE CHALLENGE. NO MATTER WHAT. WE ALWAYS--
GAG
--DELIVER AND...
AND NEVER GIVE UP!
YOU DID GOOD, KID.
MAYBE ONLY L-L-L-L-LEVEL UP ONCE PER ADVENTURE FROM NOW ON, COOL?

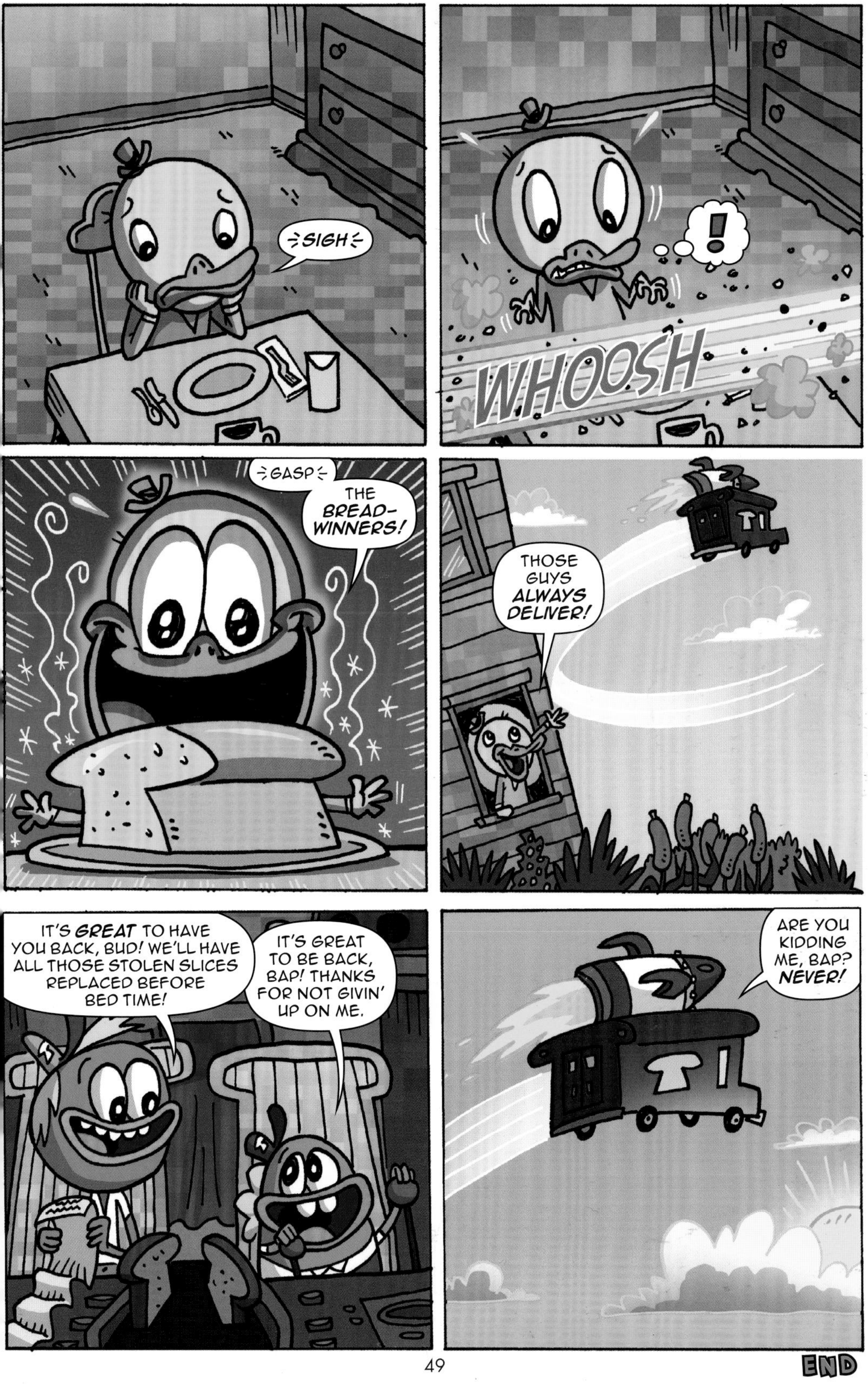
SIGH
!
WHOOSH
GASP
THE BREAD-WINNERS!
THOSE GUYS ALWAYS DELIVER!
IT'S GREAT TO HAVE YOU BACK, BUD! WE'LL HAVE ALL THOSE STOLEN SLICES REPLACED BEFORE BED TIME!
IT'S GREAT TO BE BACK, BAP! THANKS FOR NOT GIVIN' UP ON ME.
ARE YOU KIDDING ME, BAP? NEVER!
END

Ever wonder who came up with your favorite Nickelodeon characters?
NICKELODEON PANDEMONIUM #1 featured a mini-interview with BREADWINNERS co-creator Steve Borst.
Guess who we mini-interview now?

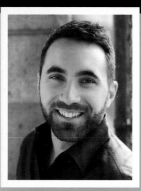

Here's BREADWINNERS Co-creator

GARY "DOODLES" DIRAFFAELE

BREADWINNERS

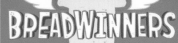

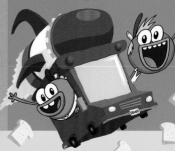

Papercutz: *Did you ever watch cartoons or read comics as a kid?*
Gary Doodles: Of course! I watched tons of cartoons. Probably too many. When I wasn't watching them, I was drawing them in my sketch book and coming up with characters of my own.
Papercutz: *What were your favorites?*
Gary Doodles: THE SIMPSONS, TEENAGE MUTANT NINJA TURTLES, HE-MAN, THUNDERCATS, REN AND STIMPY.

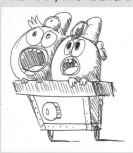

Papercutz: *What inspired you to start animating cartoons?*
Gary Doodles: A lot of things! Movies, video games, cartoons, music, sandwiches, animation. I love the creative process. I love making things. I used to make cartoons on paper using a pencil, which took forever! But once technology advanced to the point where you can make a cartoon on your home computer, that's when I really started getting more into animating my own cartoons. Computers are powerful machines, you can use them to do a lot of cool things like researching history, connecting with the world, ordering pizza, or making cartoons! An animation program called Adobe Flash (now called Adobe Animate) changed the way I made cartoons. I still use it to this day and it's way faster than using paper and pencil. I encourage anyone who wants to make cartoons to learn an animation program like Flash and start making cartoons! A Wacom Cintiq or Tablet makes it easy to draw straight into the computer. Good luck, my ducky ducks!
Papercutz: *How did you meet BREADWINNERS co-creator Steve Borst and what made you interested in working with him in making BREADWINNERS?*
Gary Doodles: I met Steve [Borst] while working on a cartoon show called MAD. I remember it like it was YEASTerday... there we were, hanging out next to a copy machine. We spoke about the weather, how cool Friday's are, and how much we like cartoons. Steve really liked writing cartoons, and I really liked animating cartoons, so we decided to join forces and make a cartoon! A few months later, BREADWINNERS was born.
Papercutz: *What was the concept behind BREADWINNERS?*

BREADHOUSE

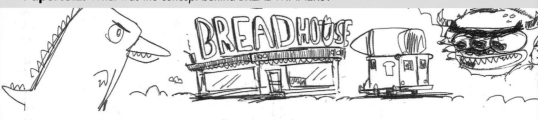

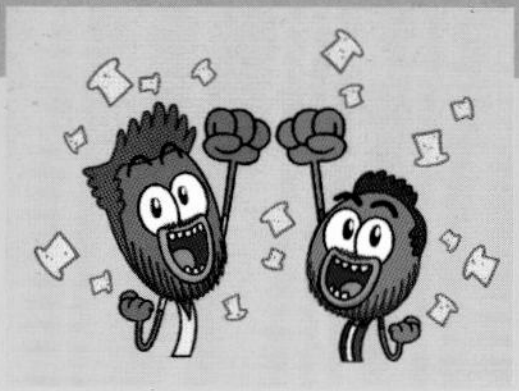

Gary Doodles: At its core, Breadwinners is about two best friend ducks named SwaySway and Buhdeuce who deliver bread in a high powered Rocket Van.

Papercutz: *What's the process behind animating a story?*

Gary Doodles: It's complicated, so buckle up duckies! It all starts at Nickelodeon Animation Studios in Burbank, California, where our creative team collaborates to bring these quazy characters to life. Once the script is written and approved, we record the voice actors saying all the lines written in the script. We then make a Radio Play, in which all of the actors' dialogue is edited in the computer and is timed out to a rhythmic beat with added sound effects and music. Think of a Radio Play like you were watching the cartoon, but without any picture, just sound! The Radio Play is then used as a guide for the storyboard team to draw to. The storyboard artists draw characters in specific poses based on the direction of the script and story. Once the storyboard is complete we render out an Animatic, which is basically a black and white rough version of the cartoon. We then edit the episode to approximately 10:45 minutes. At this point we are ready to ship the episode to an animation studio called Titmouse located in Vancouver, Canada where the animation is produced. Titmouse has dozens of talented artists and animators who bring the story to life using hi-tech digital computers. Once the animation is completed, we mix the final picture to the final dialogue, sound effects and music at a post production house called Atlas Oceanic back in Burbank. After the episode is mixed, we send it off to the network for final televised broadcast. Keep in mind, there are multiple revisions at each stage of the process to make the story stronger, the jokes funnier, and the artwork as amazing as possible. It takes a lot of dedicated people to make an episode of Breadwinners. Just like SwaySway and Buhdeuce take a lot of pride delivering their fresh bread to their customers, we all take a lot of pride delivering funny episodes to our audience.

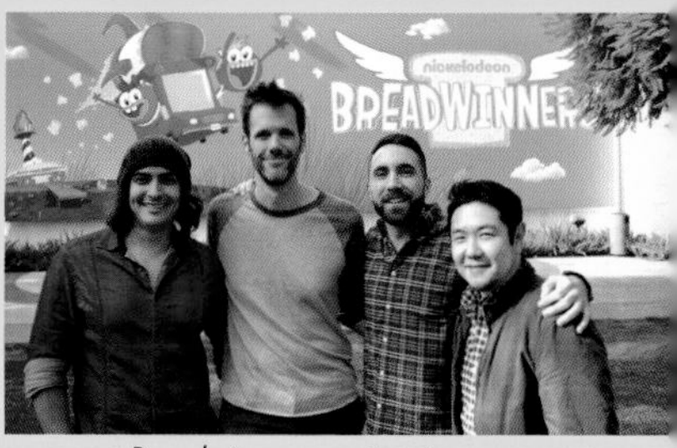
BREADWINNER
Breadwinners creators team

Papercutz: *What were the original concepts behind SwaySway and Buhdeuce?*

Gary Doodles: When I was designing these bread lovin' ducks, I wanted them to look iconic, simple, and appealing. I felt Sway should be tall and cool because he is the leader. Buhdeuce is a Breadwinner in training and looks up to Sway, so I made him short and goofy. They treat each other like family; however, they are brothers from another mother.

Papercutz: *What was the concept behind the world of Breadwinners?*

Gary Doodles: Since SwaySway and Buhdeuce are ducks, and ducks live around ponds, we felt like they should live on a pond-based planet. We dubbed their planet Pondgea, inspired by the historic supercontinent Pangea. Any creatures you'd find in or around a pond you would find on Pondgea, like beavers, frogs, toads and ducks. But we also wanted to add a threat to our main characters, something that would make delivering bread extra dangerous. So we added bread hungry Pond Monsters that lurk under the water waiting to snatch up the Breadwinner's bread at any moment. We also have Cave Monsters down in the Bread Mines and Cloud Monsters high up in the sky too. No matter where these ducks go, they've got to watch their tail feathers or they just might end up roast meat!

Papercutz: *Do you really like bread? How did it become a big part of Breadwinners?*

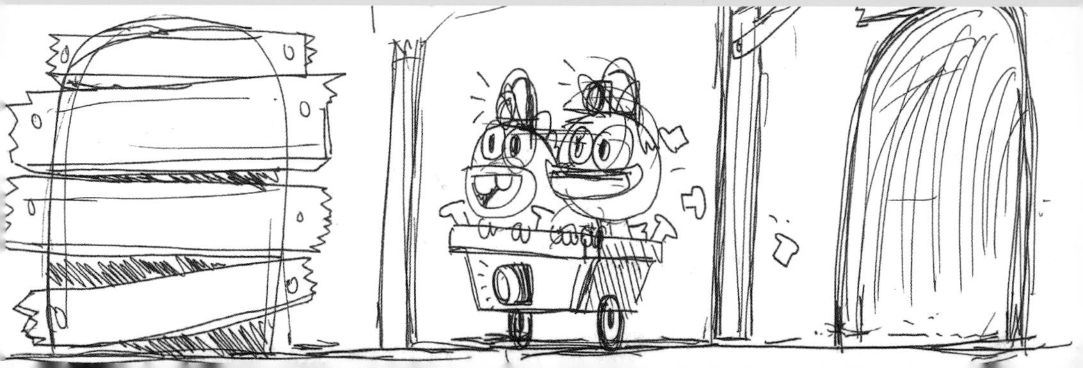

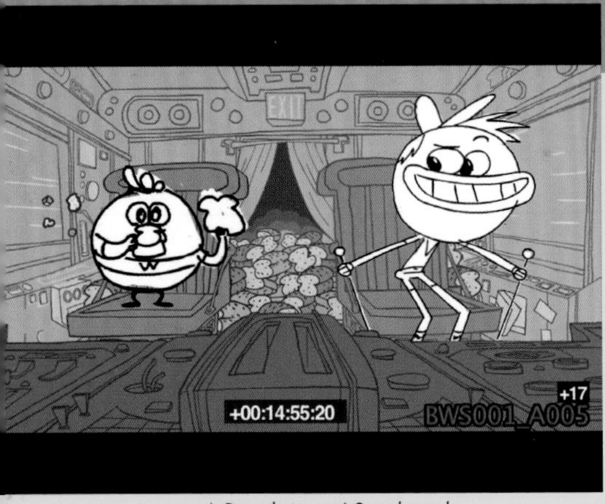
EXIT
+00:14:55:20
+17
BWS001_A005
A Breadwinners' Storyboard

Gary Doodles: Yes. Bread and I go way back. We have an inseparable bond. When I was a child, my family and I used to feed loaves of bread to ducks at the local pond. I witnessed ducks of all shapes and sizes come out of the water to taste this amazing carbohydrate. From crumbs to crusts these webbed creatures loved bread just as much as me! In Breadwinners, since the planet was inhabited by a large population of ducks, it made sense to my 3 year old self, that all ducks need to eat bread! Cartoons are supposed to be silly and wacky, and because we created a wacky world, we don't have to be true to science.

Papercutz: *Why did you make SwaySway and Buhdeuce bread deliverymen?*

Gary Doodles: It's what Breadwinners do: they deliver bread! It's part of their job, and what better job to have if you are a duck who loves bread?

Papercutz: *Who's your favorite character in the series and why?*

Gary Doodles: The Bread Maker! Because he is a cool crusty dude who makes all the BREADonkulous bread for the entire planet.

Papercutz: *Which character do you relate to the most in the series and why?*

Gary Doodles: SwaySway! Because he's resilient, fearless, loves bread and takes pride in his work. I also admire his dedication to party punching as well as his ability to crash land the Rocket Van with great expertise.

Papercutz: *Would you ever want to work with SwaySway and Buhdeuce and why or why not?*

Gary Doodles: YES! Working with those bread-heads would be super sweet because it wouldn't even feel like work, because Breadwinning is so much fun. We would do barrel rolls in the Rocket Van, outrun bread chomping monsters in the Bread Mines, make bread with the Bread Maker, eat loaves of freshly mined bread with the Bread Maker, party punch all day long. There are too many reasons to work with those baps!

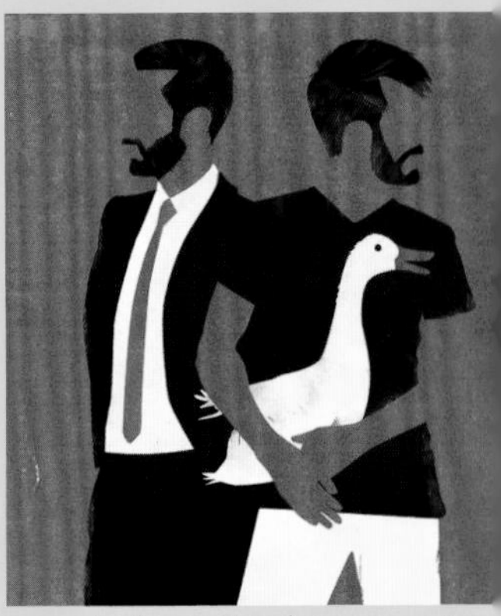
Duck-tastic Breadwinners creators

Papercutz: *How did you feel when you found out that Breadwinners was going to be a full-length series?*

Gary Doodles: When I found out Breadwinners was going to be a series I was like, "Oh! My! Bap!" and then my head exploded! Seriously, it was mind blowing news! I love making cartoons, so to make a cartoon on a series scale was something I always wanted to experience first hand as an animator. And because I watched a ton of Nickelodeon cartoons growing up, this was the perfect opportunity to inspire and entertain a brand new generation of kids.

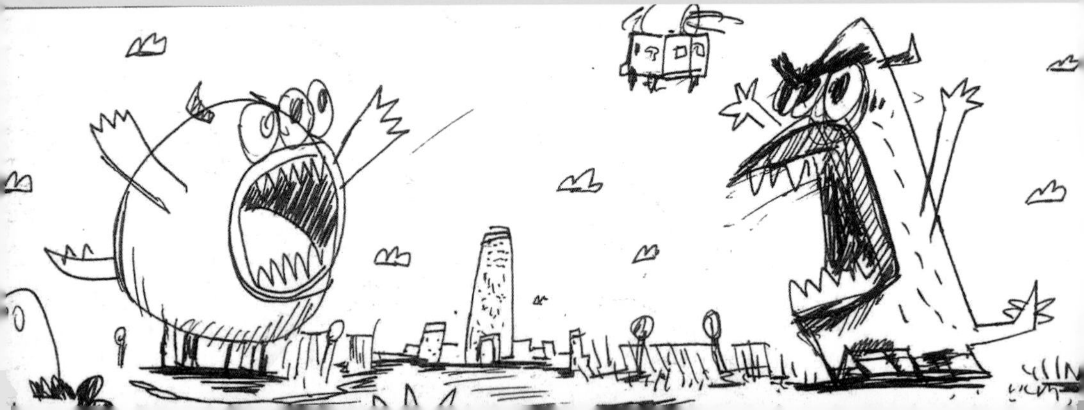

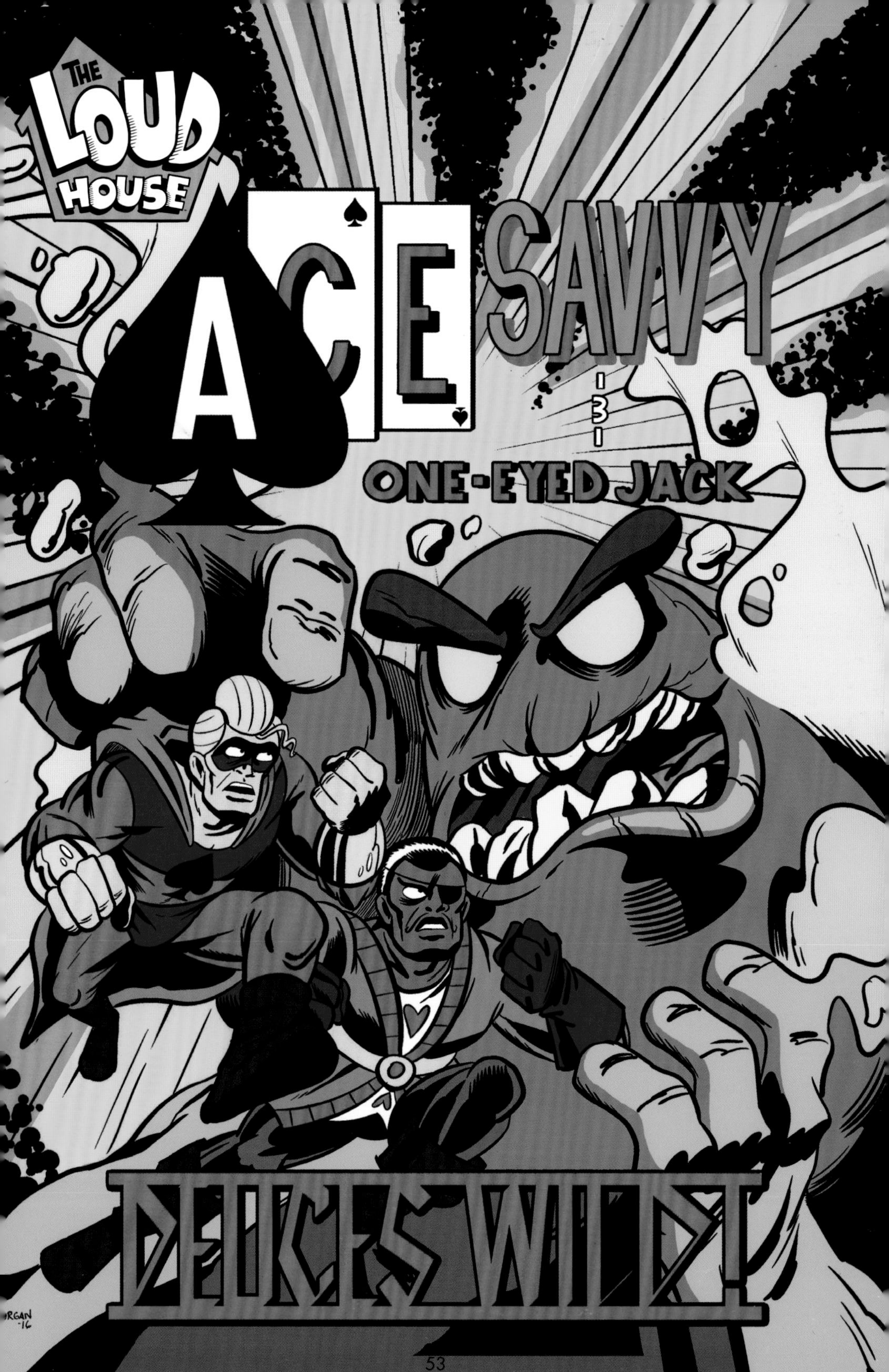
THE LOUD HOUSE
ACE SAVVY
ONE-EYED JACK
DEUCES WILD!

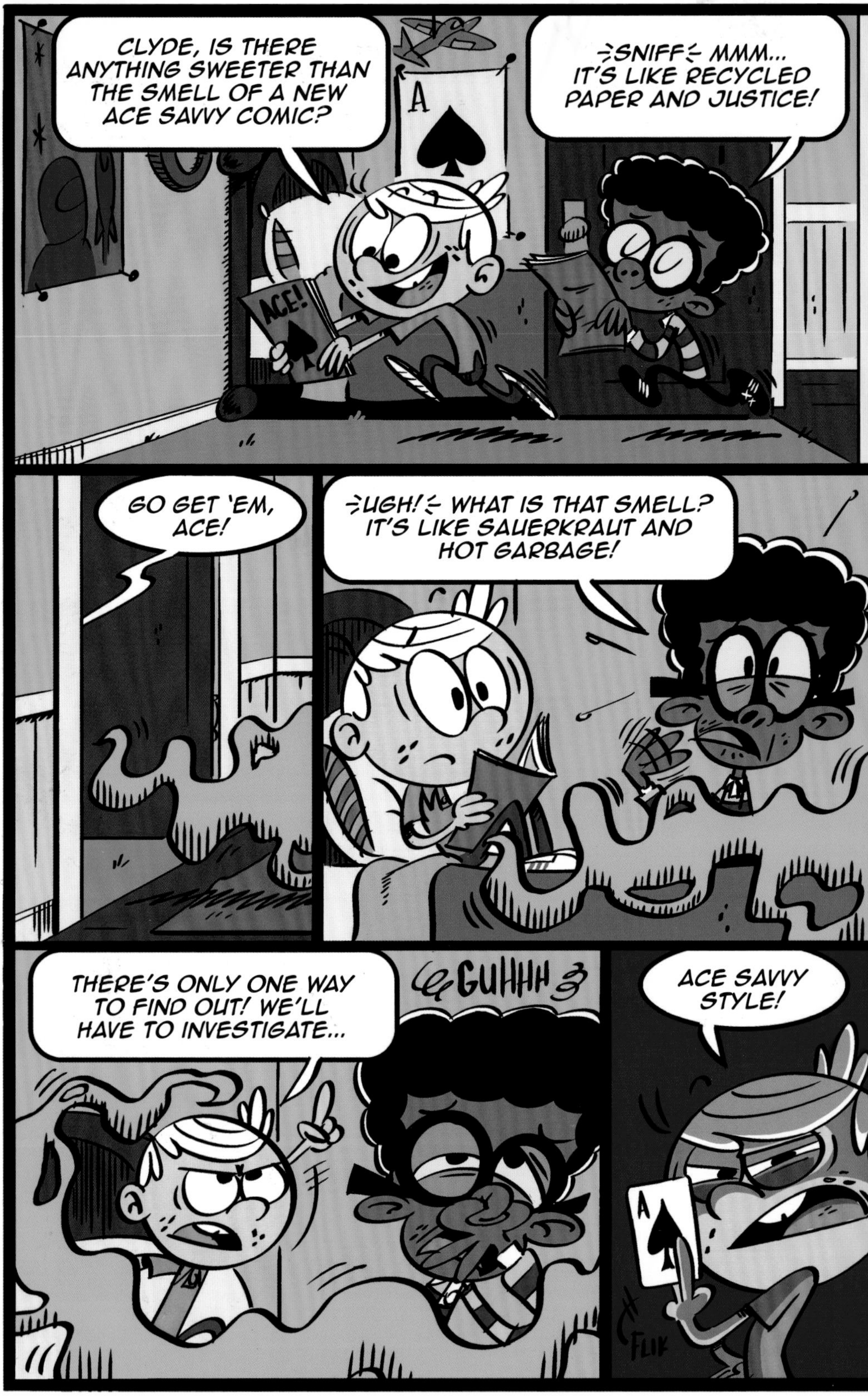
CLYDE, IS THERE ANYTHING SWEETER THAN THE SMELL OF A NEW ACE SAVVY COMIC?
ACE!
SNIFF MMM... IT'S LIKE RECYCLED PAPER AND JUSTICE!
GO GET 'EM, ACE!
UGH! WHAT IS THAT SMELL? IT'S LIKE SAUERKRAUT AND HOT GARBAGE!
THERE'S ONLY ONE WAY TO FIND OUT! WE'LL HAVE TO INVESTIGATE...
GUHHH
ACE SAVVY STYLE!
FLIK

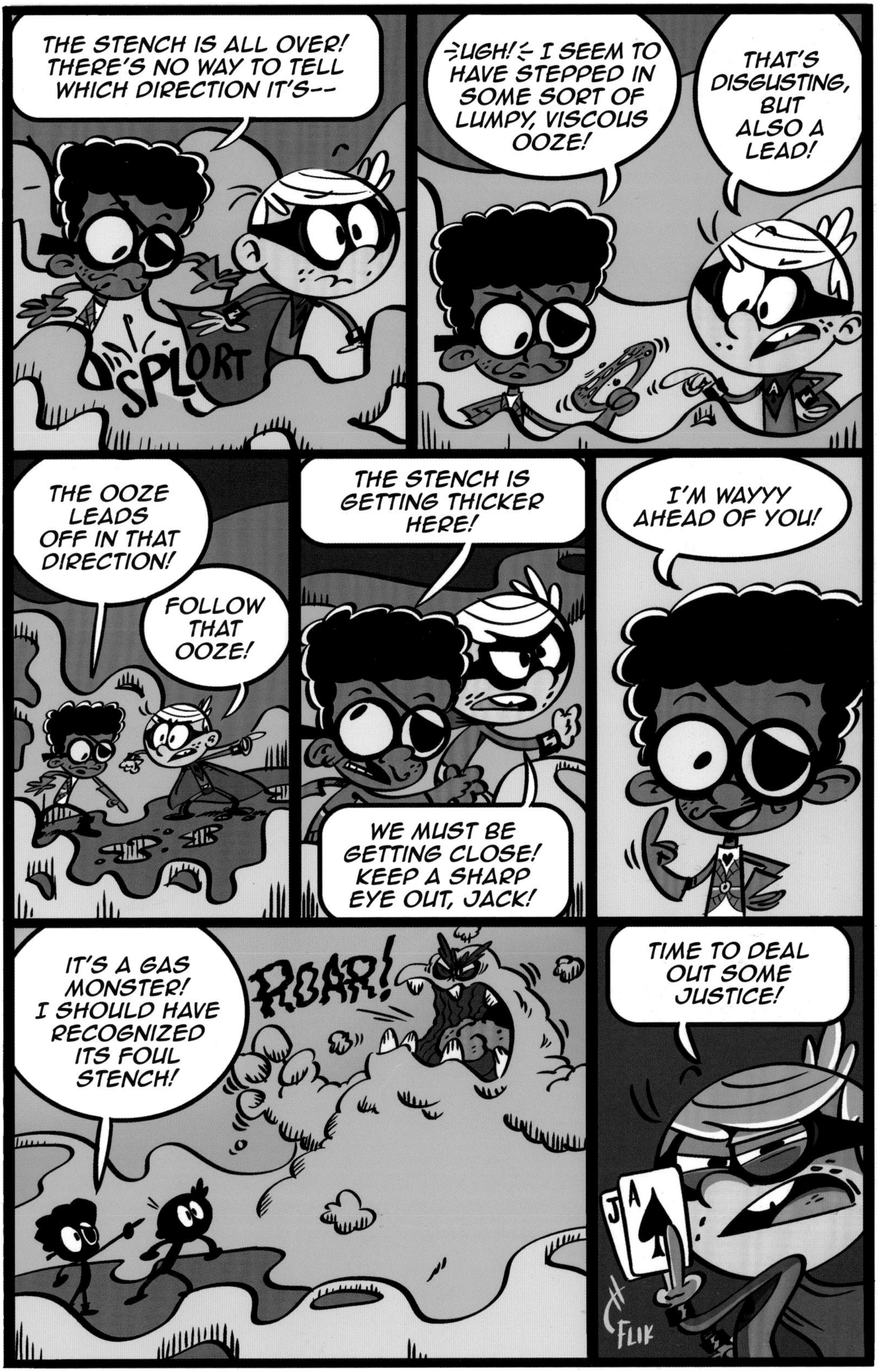
THE STENCH IS ALL OVER! THERE'S NO WAY TO TELL WHICH DIRECTION IT'S--
SPLORT
UGH! I SEEM TO HAVE STEPPED IN SOME SORT OF LUMPY, VISCOUS OOZE!
THAT'S DISGUSTING, BUT ALSO A LEAD!
THE OOZE LEADS OFF IN THAT DIRECTION!
FOLLOW THAT OOZE!
THE STENCH IS GETTING THICKER HERE!
WE MUST BE GETTING CLOSE! KEEP A SHARP EYE OUT, JACK!
I'M WAYYY AHEAD OF YOU!
IT'S A GAS MONSTER! I SHOULD HAVE RECOGNIZED ITS FOUL STENCH!
ROAR!
TIME TO DEAL OUT SOME JUSTICE!
FLIK

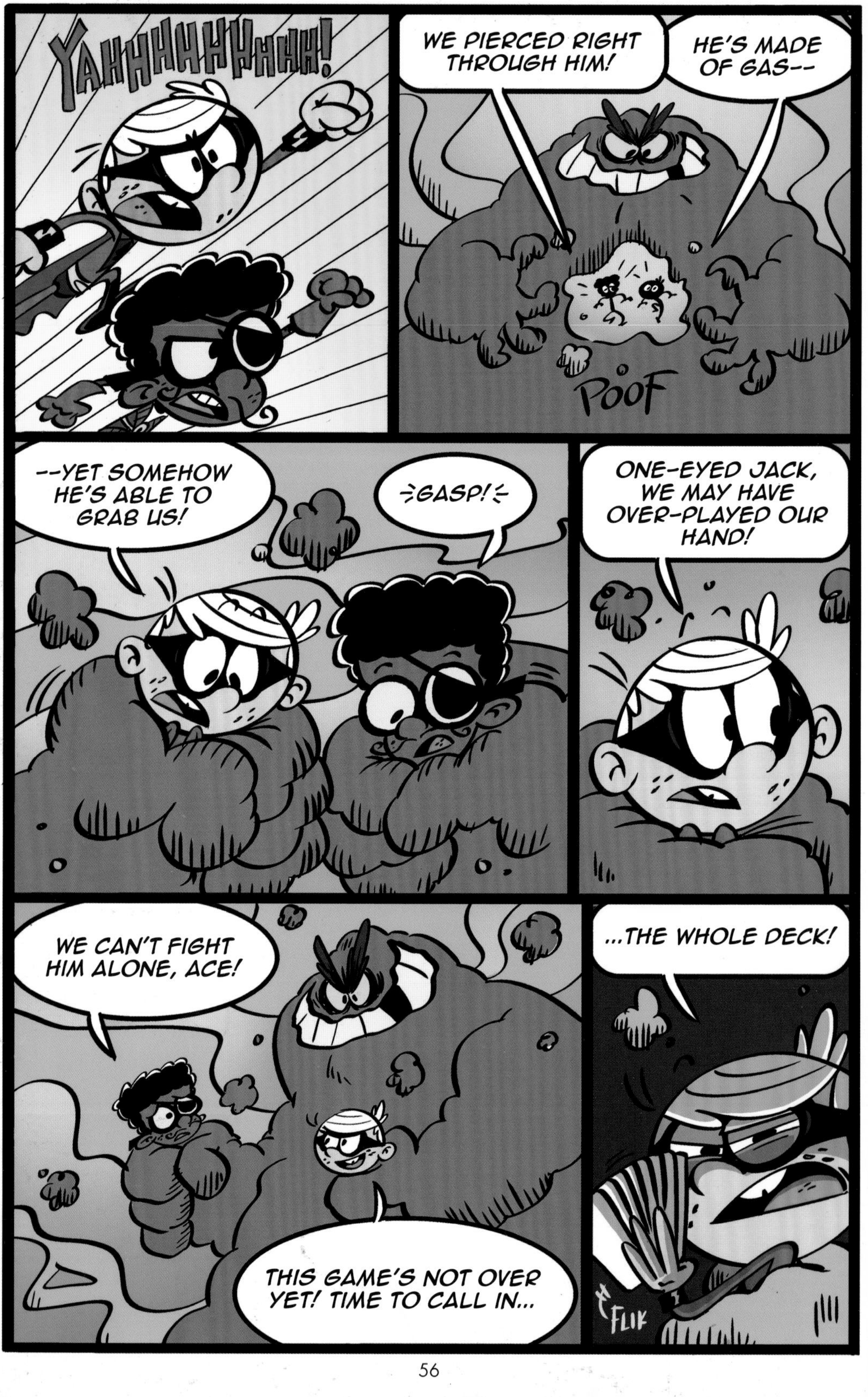
YAHHHHHHHHH!
WE PIERCED RIGHT THROUGH HIM!
HE'S MADE OF GAS--
POOF
--YET SOMEHOW HE'S ABLE TO GRAB US!
GASP!
ONE-EYED JACK, WE MAY HAVE OVER-PLAYED OUR HAND!
WE CAN'T FIGHT HIM ALONE, ACE!
THIS GAME'S NOT OVER YET! TIME TO CALL IN...
...THE WHOLE DECK!
FLIK

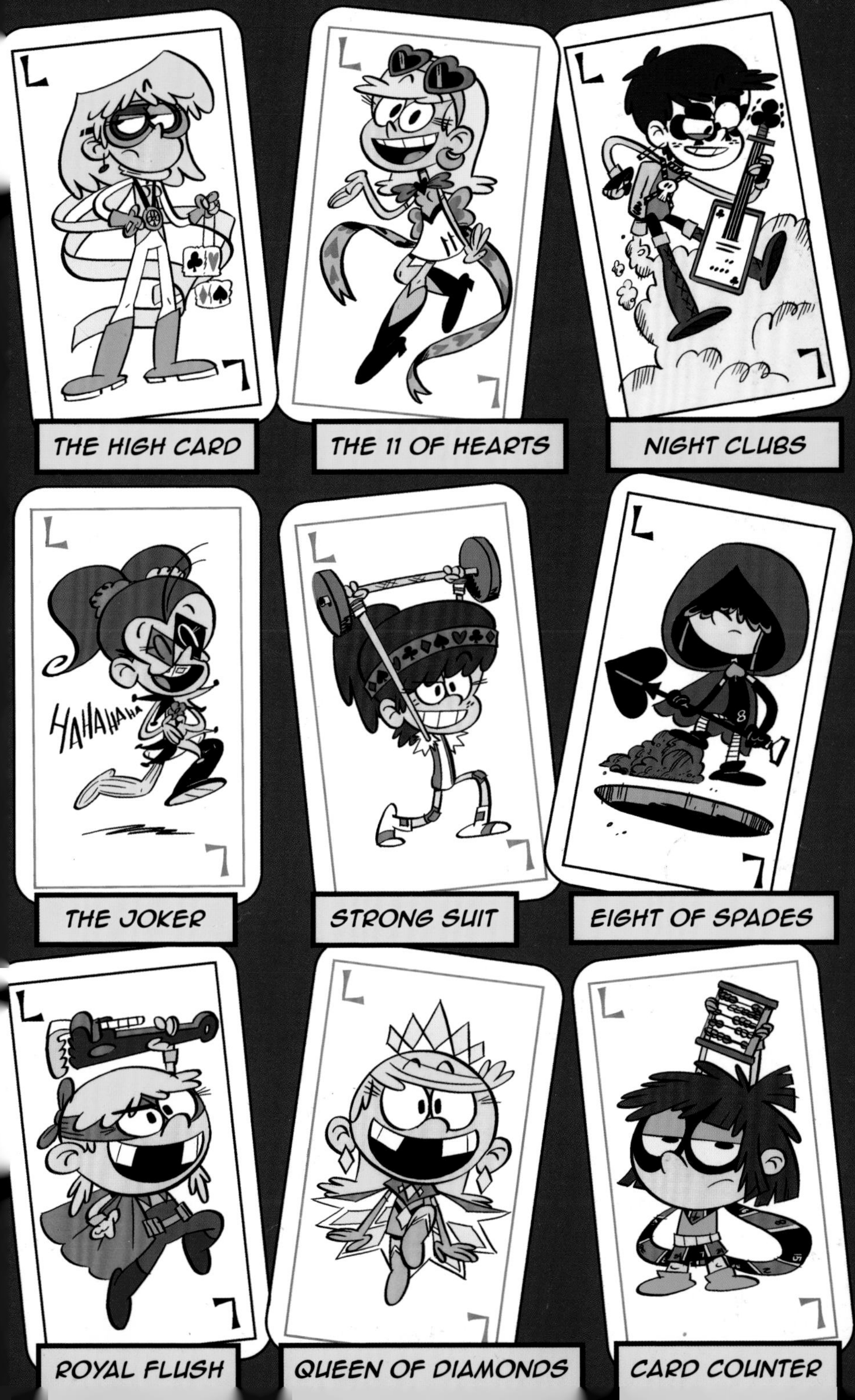
THE HIGH CARD
THE 11 OF HEARTS
NIGHT CLUBS
HAHAHAHA
THE JOKER
STRONG SUIT
EIGHT OF SPADES
ROYAL FLUSH
QUEEN OF DIAMONDS
CARD COUNTER

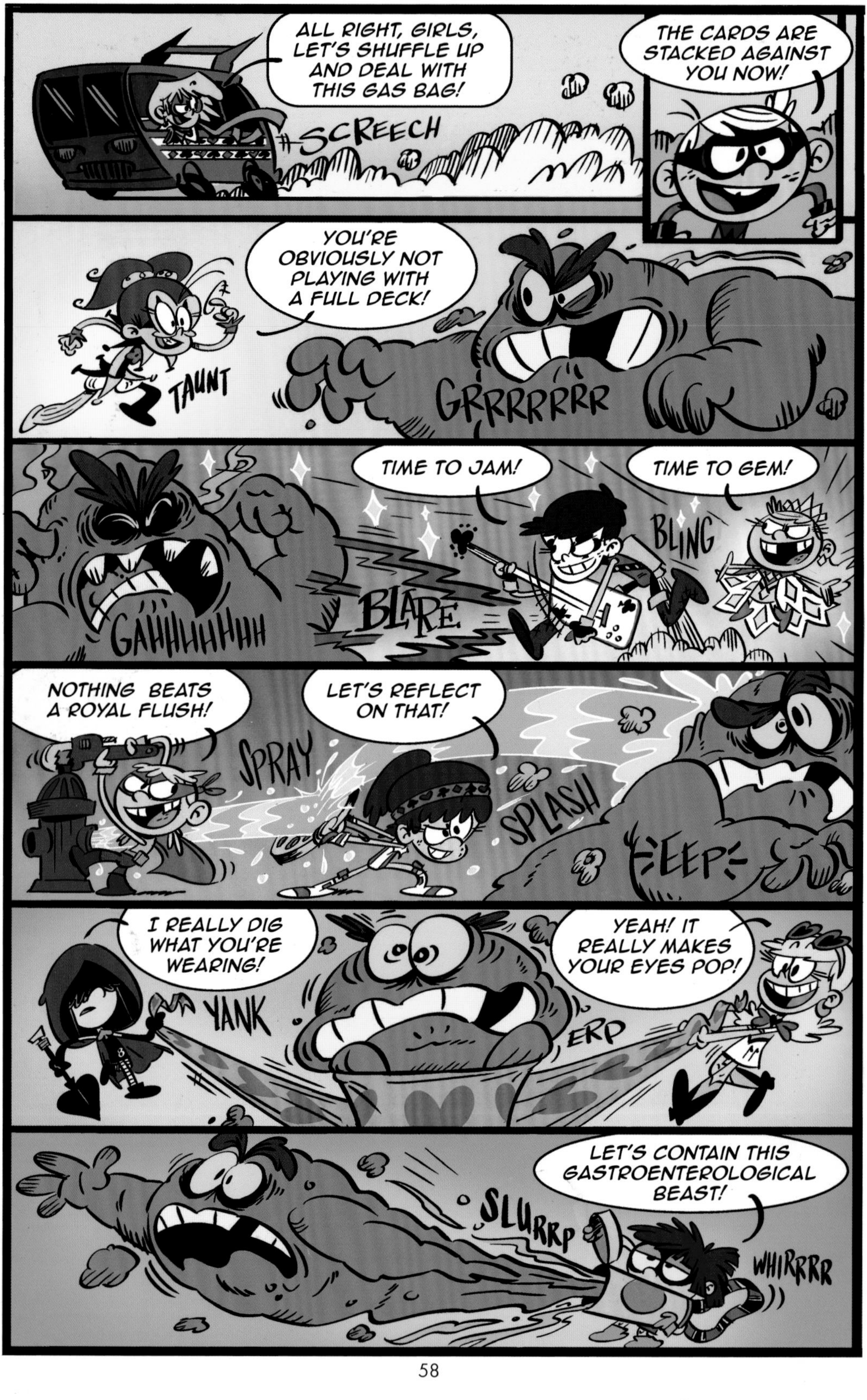
ALL RIGHT, GIRLS, LET'S SHUFFLE UP AND DEAL WITH THIS GAS BAG!
SCREECH
THE CARDS ARE STACKED AGAINST YOU NOW!
YOU'RE OBVIOUSLY NOT PLAYING WITH A FULL DECK!
TAUNT
GRRRRRRR
TIME TO JAM!
TIME TO GEM!
BLING
BLARE
GAHHHHHHH
NOTHING BEATS A ROYAL FLUSH!
LET'S REFLECT ON THAT!
SPRAY
SPLASH
EEP
I REALLY DIG WHAT YOU'RE WEARING!
YANK
YEAH! IT REALLY MAKES YOUR EYES POP!
ERP
LET'S CONTAIN THIS GASTROENTEROLOGICAL BEAST!
SLURRP
WHIRRRR

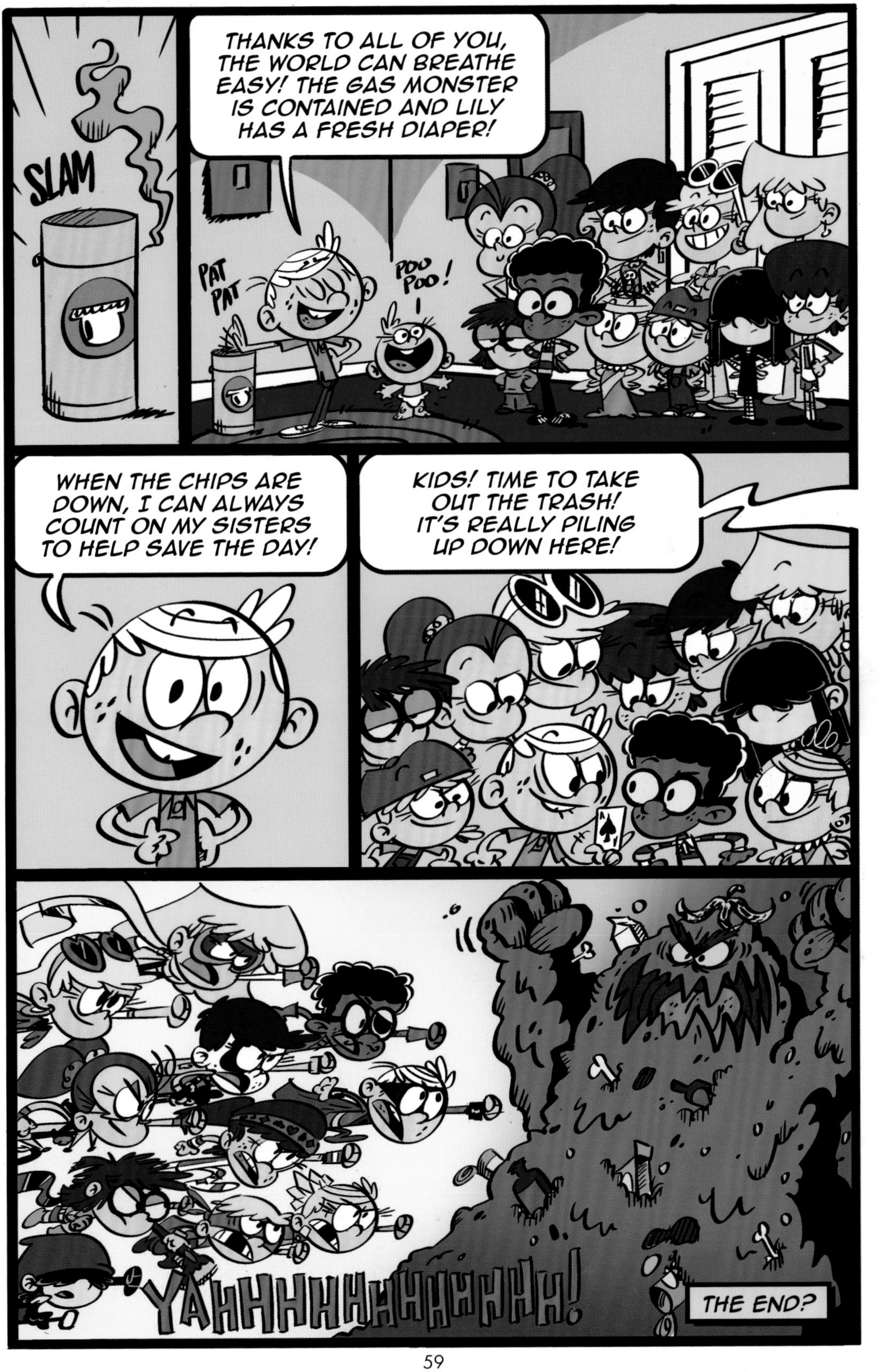
SLAM
THANKS TO ALL OF YOU, THE WORLD CAN BREATHE EASY! THE GAS MONSTER IS CONTAINED AND LILY HAS A FRESH DIAPER!
PAT PAT
POO POO!
WHEN THE CHIPS ARE DOWN, I CAN ALWAYS COUNT ON MY SISTERS TO HELP SAVE THE DAY!
KIDS! TIME TO TAKE OUT THE TRASH! IT'S REALLY PILING UP DOWN HERE!
YAHHHHHHHHHHHHH!
THE END?

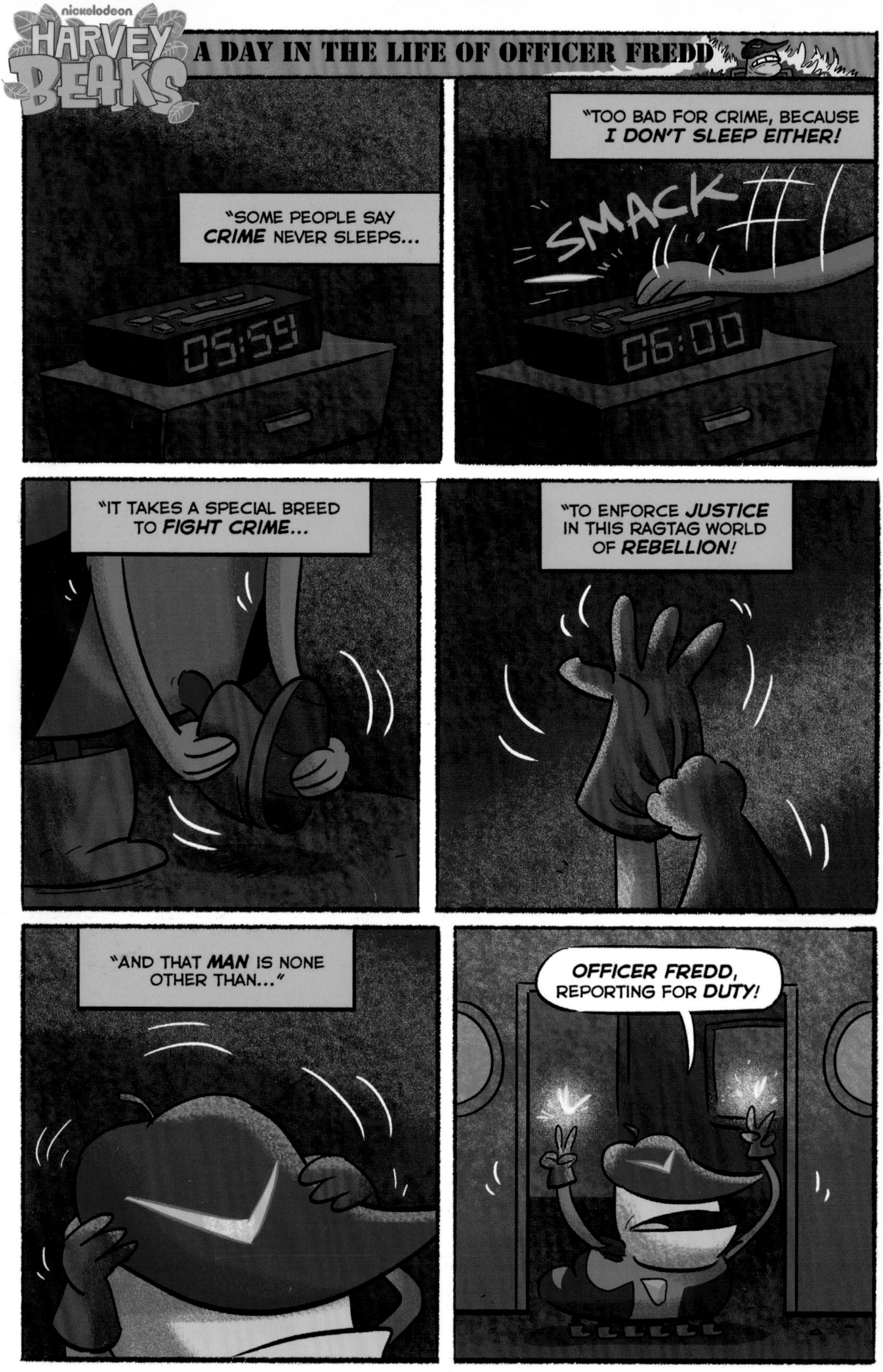
A DAY IN THE LIFE OF OFFICER FREDD
"SOME PEOPLE SAY *CRIME* NEVER SLEEPS...
05:59
"TOO BAD FOR CRIME, BECAUSE *I DON'T SLEEP EITHER!*
SMACK
06:00
"IT TAKES A SPECIAL BREED TO *FIGHT CRIME*...
"TO ENFORCE *JUSTICE* IN THIS RAGTAG WORLD OF *REBELLION*!
"AND THAT *MAN* IS NONE OTHER THAN..."
OFFICER FREDD, REPORTING FOR *DUTY*!

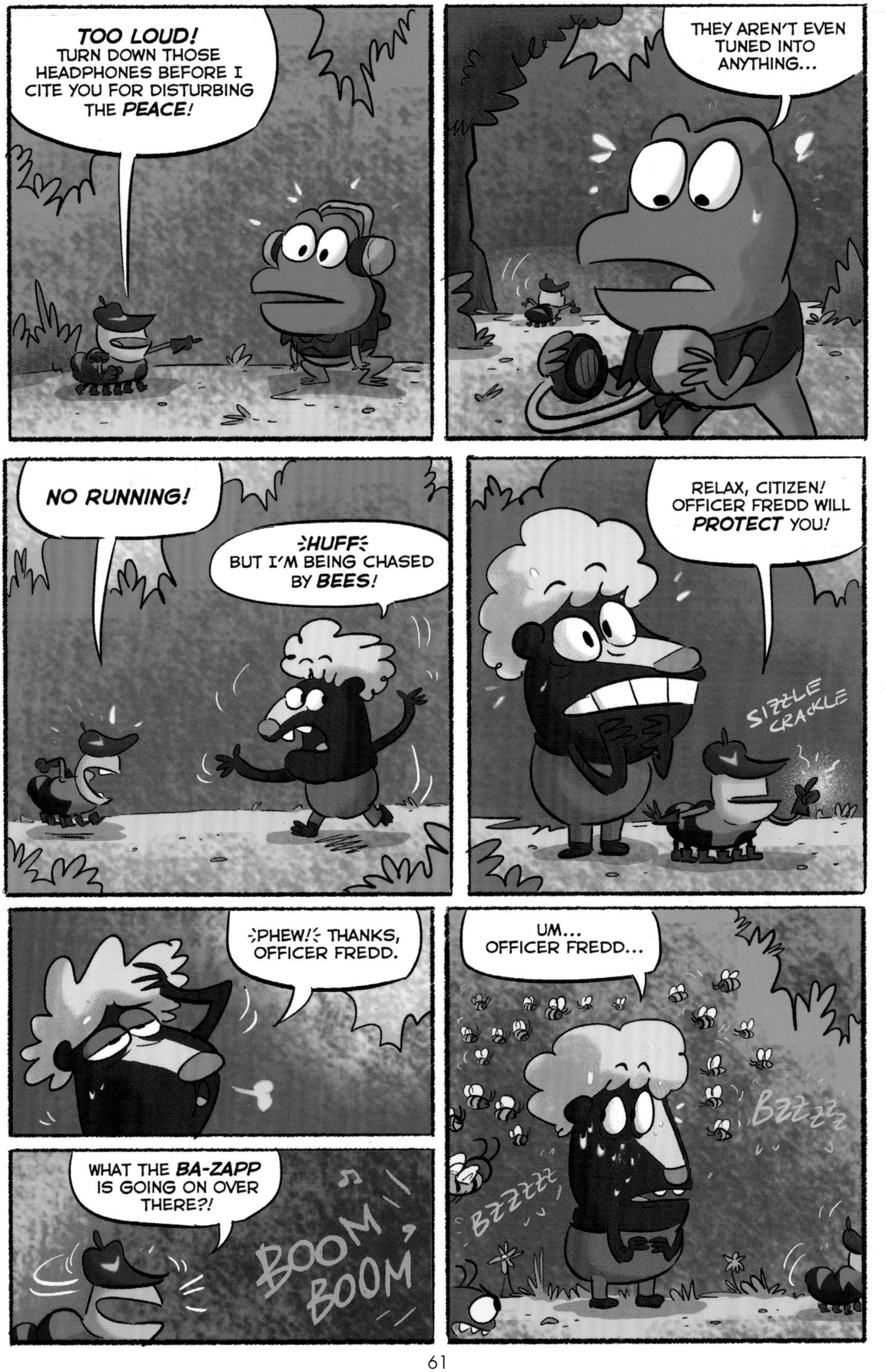
TOO LOUD! TURN DOWN THOSE HEADPHONES BEFORE I CITE YOU FOR DISTURBING THE PEACE!
THEY AREN'T EVEN TUNED INTO ANYTHING...
NO RUNNING!
HUFF BUT I'M BEING CHASED BY BEES!
RELAX, CITIZEN! OFFICER FREDD WILL PROTECT YOU!
SIZZLE CRACKLE
PHEW! THANKS, OFFICER FREDD.
WHAT THE BA-ZAPP IS GOING ON OVER THERE?!
BOOM BOOM
UM... OFFICER FREDD...
Bzzzzz
BZZZZZ

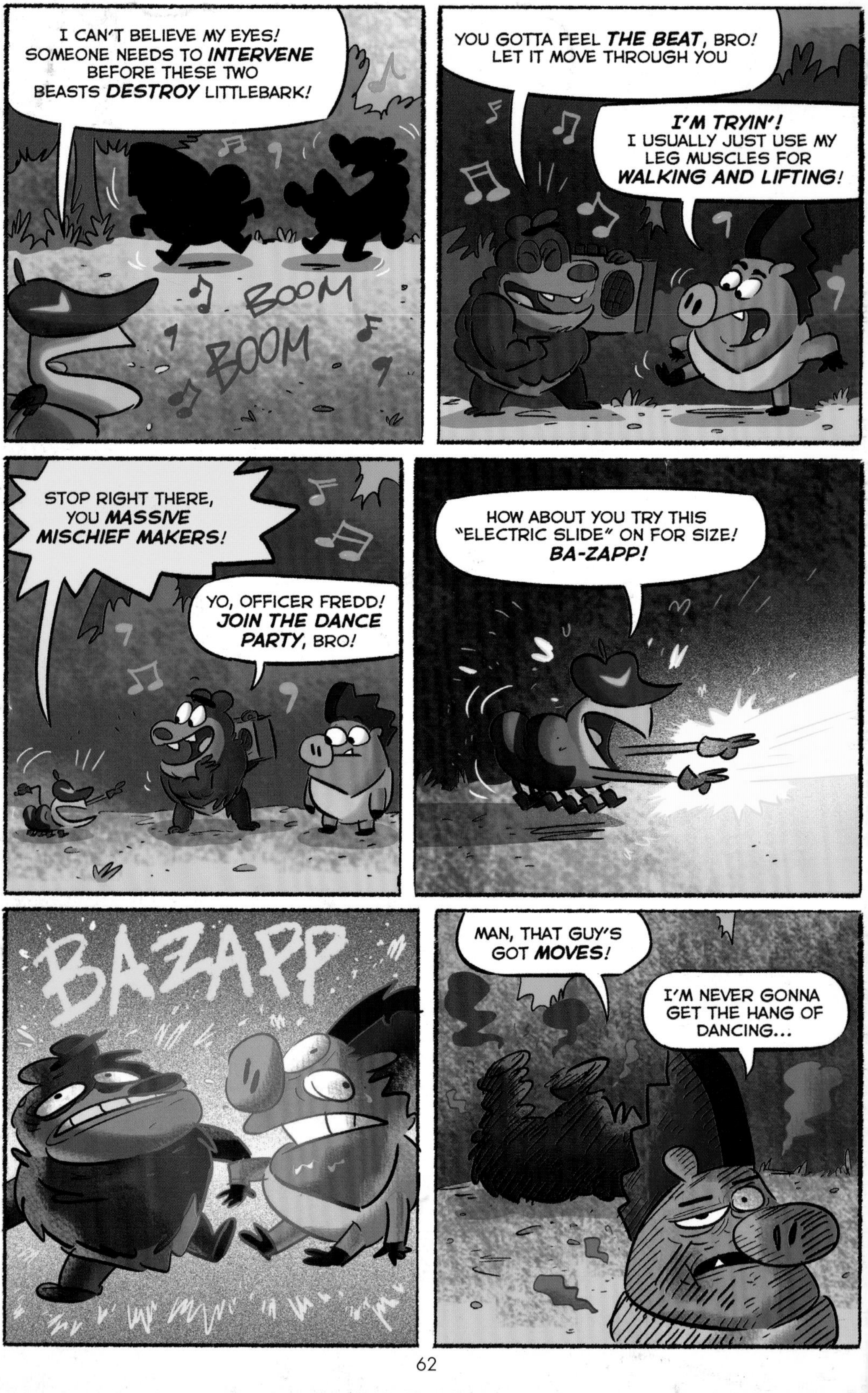
I CAN'T BELIEVE MY EYES! SOMEONE NEEDS TO INTERVENE BEFORE THESE TWO BEASTS DESTROY LITTLEBARK!
BOOM
BOOM
YOU GOTTA FEEL THE BEAT, BRO! LET IT MOVE THROUGH YOU
I'M TRYIN'! I USUALLY JUST USE MY LEG MUSCLES FOR WALKING AND LIFTING!
STOP RIGHT THERE, YOU MASSIVE MISCHIEF MAKERS!
YO, OFFICER FREDD! JOIN THE DANCE PARTY, BRO!
HOW ABOUT YOU TRY THIS "ELECTRIC SLIDE" ON FOR SIZE! BA-ZAPP!
BAZAPP
MAN, THAT GUY'S GOT MOVES!
I'M NEVER GONNA GET THE HANG OF DANCING...

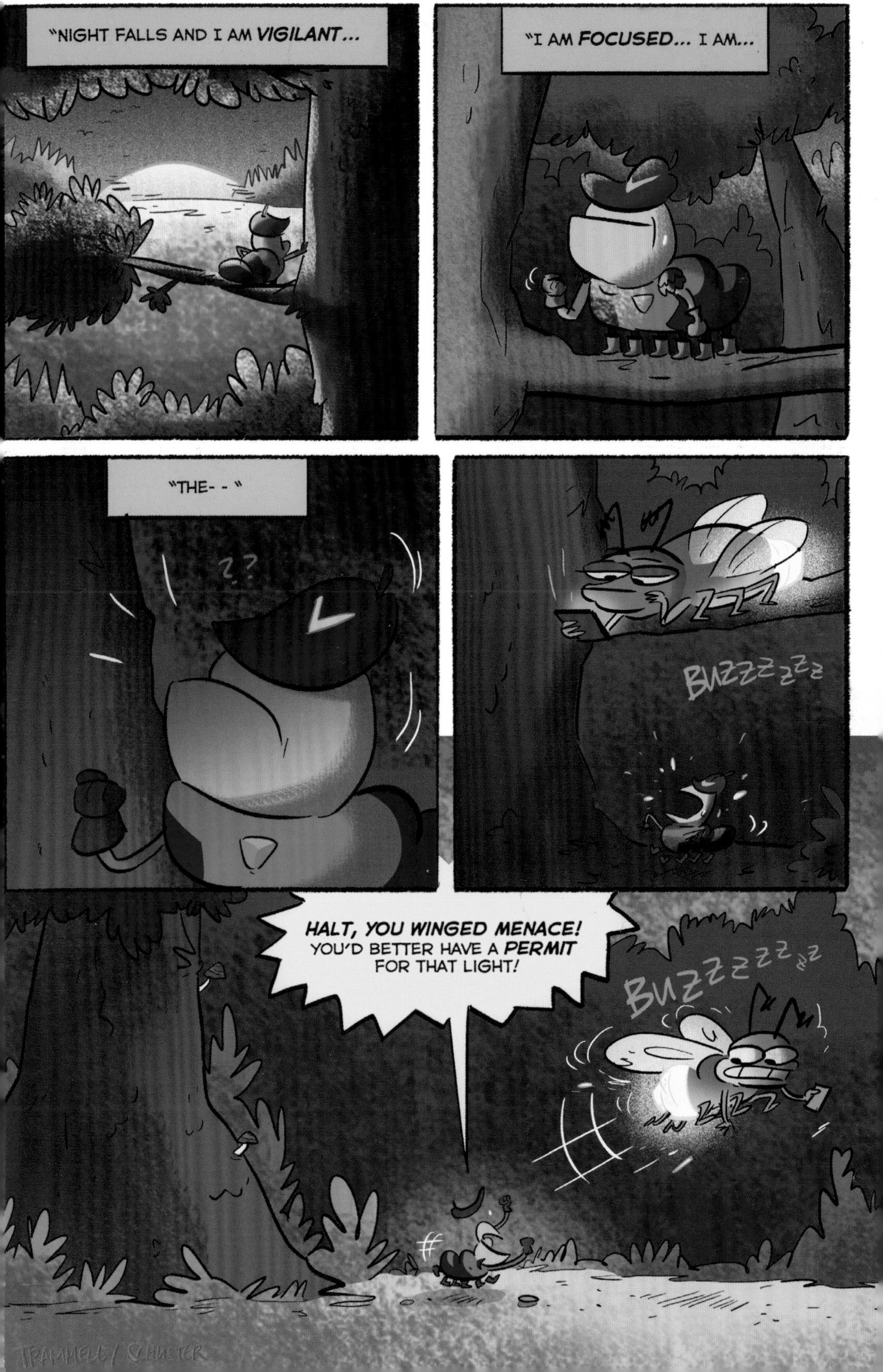
"NIGHT FALLS AND I AM VIGILANT...
"I AM FOCUSED... I AM...
"THE- - "
??
BUZZZZZZ
HALT, YOU WINGED MENACE! YOU'D BETTER HAVE A PERMIT FOR THAT LIGHT!
BUZZZZZZZZ
TRAMMELL / SCHUSTER

WATCH OUT FOR PAPERCUTZ

Welcome to the spy-filled (and sleuthing-ducktective-featuring) second NICKELODEON PANDEMONIUM! graphic novel from Papercutz (AKA **P**rofessional **A**rtists **P**reparing **E**ditorially **R**equested **C**omics **U**ncovering **T**remendous **Z**aniness), that (worst-kept) secret organization dedicated to releasing to the general population (after Freedom of Info-tainment Act requests have been filed at various locations code-named "bookstores" and/or "comic shops") extremely well-executed graphic novels for all possible purchasers. I'm James, James Salicrup, otherwise known as "Jim," the Organization's Chief of Editors. Overtly operating out of what seems to be a company offering seemingly harmless funny comics either in print or digitally, our real mission is far more covert, in that we are providing inspired entertainment to enrich the minds of countless potential world leaders and important decision-makers (AKA you!).

In other words, we've gone to a lot of trouble to get the following top secret message to you. We had to seek out the most sophisticated and intelligent operatives by putting together this graphic novel featuring the coolest characters created in the last few years. It's specifically designed for someone who can appreciate the cautious courage of Harvey Beaks– compared to the rowdy recklessness of Fee and Foo. Carefully crafted to appeal to someone who cannot be thrown by the unlikely combinations of Pig Goat Banana Cricket, or Sanjay and Craig, but who can see their effective and tenacious teamwork. Relentlessly researched to include just the right ingredients to attract someone who embraces the can-do spirit of SwaySway and Buhdeuce, the indefatigable Breadwinners. And brilliantly conceived to pull in someone who, like Lincoln Loud, can retain their own identity despite great pressure from others. Yes, we're looking to you to become an agent of P.A.P.E.R.C.U.T.Z.!

Your mission, if you choose to accept it, is a simple one. We're looking to you to enlist others like yourself, others who can appreciate the comics and characters found in NICKELODEON PANDEMONIUM! to join the ever-growing ranks of P.A.P.E.R.C.U.T.Z. Full disclosure: There is some risk involved. Sometimes merely telling a friend how much you enjoy NICKELODEON PANDEMONIUM! is all that is required. But there have been cases where it took a little more— like actually loaning out your prized NICKELODEON PANDEMONIUM! graphic novel, so that its greatness can more easily be seen and understood. While it is rare, there have been cases of those NICKELODEON PANDEMONIUM graphic novels never being returned.

The preceding message will self-destruct in several hundred years. So, get smart and safeguard this graphic novel on your favorite bookshelf in your safe house. It's not an impossible mission.

Be on the lookout for future missions in NICKELODEON PANEMONIUM! #3 "Nick or Treat?" But be warned, the message may be encrypted and look like an incredibly funny Halloween-themed comics story featuring Nickelodeon super-stars. We're clever like that!

Good luck,

Jim

(Formerly Agent Double Uh-oh Seven)

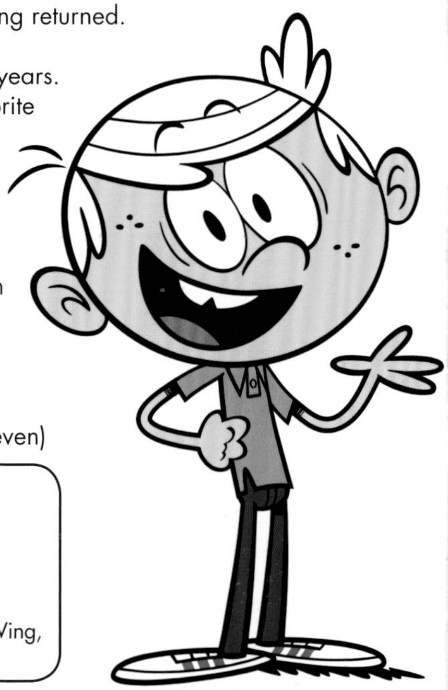

STAY IN TOUCH!

EMAIL:	salicrup@papercutz.com
WEB:	papercutz.com
TWITTER:	@papercutzgn
FACEBOOK:	PAPERCUTZGRAPHICNOVELS
FANMAIL:	Papercutz, 160 Broadway, Suite 700, East Wing, New York, NY 10038